PATCHWORK

BY DESIREE BYARS

ILLUSTRATIONS BY
MIKE L. LANE

EDITED BY
LISA LEE TONE
DONELLE PARDEE WHITING

For Stephen
Forever and a day

Contents

Bailey Marie

"Do you guys believe in abortion?"

Bailey Heron's mother dropped her fork and took a swallow of wine. Her father pushed his plate away and blew out a long breath.

"What sort of question is that for a nine-year-old?" her mother asked.

"Shouldn't be surprised, Janet," her father said. "Our little girl is well beyond her years." He beamed at his daughter.

"I just wanted to know," Bailey said, slurping up noodles.

"Lenny! We do *not* need to be having this conversation!" Her mother's hands trembled around her glass.

"Oh, come on, Janet. If she wants to know, it's better she has this discussion here at home rather than at school with a bunch of kids who learned everything off the internet."

Bailey smiled at her father. He always treated her like an adult. Her mother rarely spoke to her about anything other than chores, but the occasional conversations they did manage to have were worded to make Bailey feel small and insignificant.

"Why are you asking this?" her mom asked, clearing her throat. She looked at her empty wine glass, rose from the table, and took it into the kitchen.

Bailey looked down at her plate, swirling

her spaghetti noodles with her fork. She bit her lower lip to keep from smiling.

"Do you know what the word 'abortion' means?" her father asked.

"I know what it means," Bailey said. She looked at her mother, their brown eyes tethered to each other by invisible ropes. "It means a woman wants to kill her baby."

"Well, I suppose that's the gist of it," her father said. "Only some women don't consider it 'killing' their baby. Some women don't consider the baby—or fetus, as it's called in science—a person yet."

"Yeah," Bailey said. "But do you think it's wrong?"

Her father placed his elbow on the table and rested his chin in the palm of his hand. "Well, I don't know that it's a yes or no question, Bay. If a woman is sick, or the baby isn't going to survive ..." Her father trailed off and chewed his lip, thinking. "There are several other reasons where it might be the right choice, and then I'd understand the decision. But I don't think it should be made lightly either."

"Right, but what if she just didn't want the baby?" Bailey asked.

"Well, then no, I don't think that's right," he said.

"Should women like that be punished?" Bailey asked. Her eyes searched his, trying to telepathically transfer a message: *please say yes.*

"Punished? I don't know. That seems a harsh way to put it. I guess. Where's all this coming from, Bay? Why are you asking these questions?"

"I read a story, a real-life story, about a

mother who got pregnant, and she didn't want the baby, so she tried to abort it. No matter what she did, the kid still came anyway." She looked at her mother. Would she recognize her own words?

"And what do *you* think about it?"

Bailey didn't hesitate. "I think it's wrong to kill your kid because you don't want them. And I think they should be punished."

Her father looked to be at a loss for words.

"Remember when you used to take me to Sunday school?" Bailey asked.

"Yes, of course I do. It's been a while. Maybe you should go back."

Bailey grinned. "No, I don't want to go back. But I learned something there, from the Bible."

"What's that?"

"There's a verse in there about an eye for an eye. Like, if you steal my bread, I could steal yours too."

"Well, I don't know if that's exactly what it means. I guess in a literal sense, yeah, maybe."

"So then if a mother kills her child, I think she should die too."

Bailey's mother gasped from the sink, wine bottle still in hand. She topped off her glass, then drank it in one swallow. She lifted the bottle to her glass for another pour, and Bailey could see her hands shaking. The neck of the bottle tapped the top of the glass, sending out Morse code.

Guilty conscience? Bailey wondered.

"That's dark, kid. What kind of books are you reading?" He looked less impressed and more concerned.

"Just a book I found," she said. She stood from the table and kissed her dad on the cheek. He put an arm around her and hugged her. "I read the whole thing already."

"Well, it's not one I would have picked for you, but it makes me proud you can handle stuff like a grown-up. You're such a smart kid."

"Love you, Dad."

"Love you too, kid."

She gathered up her plate and glass and took them to the kitchen. Her mother was now drinking wine straight from the bottle.

Neither spoke to the other.

***

"It's just a book, Janet. Relax."

Bailey climbed the steps from the living room towards her bedroom. She stopped and sat on the top step, hidden from view of her parents. She was supposed to be in bed, but she wanted to know what her mother had to say after their dinner conversation.

"Just a book? Where is she getting this shit? Are you buying her these books?"

"Yes, Janet, I'm buying my nine-year-old books about abortion. That is what I'm doing." She heard him crack open a beer can.

"Well, she's getting them from somewhere." Bailey heard the familiar clink as a wine bottle kissed a wine glass.

"What do you want me to do, Jan? Lock the kid up with Berenstein Bears and Cabbage Patch dolls? That kid hasn't watched a cartoon or played with a doll in two years." He stopped for a few seconds, probably drinking his beer.

"She's not normal for her age, and I, for one, think we should nourish that. She's gonna be someone special, I know it."

"I should have expected this," her mother said. Bailey closed her eyes and imagined fire coming from her mother's eyes and smoke from her ears. She knew what was coming next.

"You always defend her. She's so perfect. She's so smart. Bailey is so great. It's all I ever hear. She's so *special.* I'm sick of it."

"It sounds like you're jealous of a child, Jan." He chuckled, and Bailey covered her mouth to keep from laughing with him.

"Jealous?" Bailey heard the wine bottle land hard on the counter. "I'm not jealous. You make it difficult to be a mother sometimes. I always have to be the bad guy, and she's your little princess who does no wrong."

"You can leave, you know," her father said.

She held her breath, again sending telepathic messages, this time to her mother. *Please say yes, please go away.*

"That was quick. May be our record time for suggesting we throw away our marriage," she said instead.

"Pack up your bags and go. Leave Bailey here."

Please!

"I can't do that, and you know it. Who would hire me, in my thirties, with no education? Your job is to take care of me, and my job is to take care of your kid when you're not around. And you're hardly ever here anymore with the hours you've been running."

"My hours? My hours are what keep this house afloat, *dear.*" The last word sounded like it was full of syrup, oozing sarcasm. Bailey clapped her hand over her mouth again to stifle a giggle. "You wouldn't be on all those high-dollar pills or drinking expensive wine if it weren't for my hours. But maybe that's what you need. Maybe I should quit so you have to quit that shit too."

"You know I need my medication," she said. Bailey thought she heard fear in her mother's voice. "And if I leave, I'm taking Bailey."

Bailey's jaw dropped. She almost ran screaming down the stairs, but self-control won over panic, and she sat, waiting.

"Like hell you are," he said.

Yay Dad! Tell her!

"Oh yes I am. And the courts will make sure I do. They never separate a mother and child."

"You sure about that, Jan? An alcoholic, pill-popping, borderline neglectful mother would win over a hard-working, honest, sober man? You really want to bet money on that?"

"Come on, Len. What do you have to take to court to prove I'm unfit? I'm here every day, taking care of Bailey while you work all day. I take her to appointments, I buy her clothes, I get her school supplies. I'm on the PTA." Bailey could hear the silent *so there* her mother wanted to add.

"Mother of the year. You're not on the PTA out of love, doll. You're on the PTA so you look good in front of the other mothers. You buy her clothes because you're obsessed with her looking better than the other kids in the school. You're all about appearances, Jan. All pretty with no substance underneath."

Bailey wanted to wear a skirt, shake pom-

poms, and cheer her father on. He was doing great, shutting her down. *Keep it up!*

Her mother said nothing.

"You just want her for the child support," he said. Bailey heard the couch squeak as he rose.

Her mother let out a small squeal. Bailey couldn't help it anymore and peeked one eye around the wall blocking the top of the stairs.

Her father was standing over her mother, his nose almost touching hers. His finger was pointed at her chest, and he was pushing so hard, Bailey noticed it made a dent in her mother's blouse.

"Let me tell you something, *Janet*. You will *never* take my child away from me. You can get that out of your mind *right now*." Bailey saw spit jump off his lips. "That child will be three times the woman you'll ever be. She's got everything you don't. So, you back off her. Do you understand?"

"You don't have to deal with her attitude when—"

He leaned forward and pressed his forehead against her mother's. "I don't care what kind of attitude she has when I'm not here. No matter how many times I tell you different, you think she's stupid. You think she doesn't know how you feel about her?" He stood upright and put his hands on his waist.

Before her mother could respond, her father continued. "You sure she doesn't have any memories of how you treated her when she was little? And even if she doesn't, you think she doesn't notice how you treat her now? You treat the kid like she's some street cat sniffing around for food. And you wonder why she favors me over you?"

The closet. She didn't remember, but she read all about it.

"I love her, that's why. And I show her every day. I may not be here all day like you are, but when I'm here, it's about her. I pay attention to her. And she can feel it. That's why she gravitates to me and *away* from you," he said.

Bailey's heart swelled until it felt like it would come out of her chest. He was right. She knew he loved her with all his heart. Bailey hoped with her whole heart someday her mother wouldn't be a problem anymore.

***

Bailey had found the journal while her mother was next door talking to Mrs. Klein. She dug it out of a chest her mother kept at the foot of her bed, hidden beneath pillows and an old quilt. She sat in the window seat, where she could see the front walk and be able to see if her mother returned.

She read.

Well, she's almost two now. I can't have anything nice because she smashes it all to hell on her little adventures through the house. The other day she shattered a vase. I left the pieces on the floor for an hour and waited for her to run through them. Maybe swallow a small piece or two. It didn't work.

Her mother wanted her to swallow shards of glass? Her eyes ran over the next several pages, finding nothing about her. Her mother talked about medications, drinking, and arguing with her father over those things. Nothing too exciting.

Except for a later entry; the date put Bailey somewhere around two and a half years old.

I put Bailey in a closet the other day. I took one of my pills so I could get some sleep without having to watch her. I left her in the dark with a sippy cup of juice and a box of crackers. She yelled for a little while, so I gave her some Benadryl. It must have knocked her out, because she was quiet for hours while I slept. When I woke up, I checked the time—I'd been out thirteen hours! Thirteen hours of glorious sleep! But then I panicked. I was afraid Lenny might have come home and found her.

I smelled her before I even got all the way to the closet. She was eating a cracker with shit on her hands. She'd shit herself and smeared some of it on the walls, her clothes, the floor. I yanked her out and ran her upstairs and bathed her. I called Lenny to check where he was—still at work, no surprise there.

I cleaned up the closet. When he got home, he said he was ready to get some sleep. Bailey took him by the hand and led him over to the closet. My heart dropped. She pointed at the door and said, "Mama said go in there." I said, "No, honey, I didn't." She nodded at Lenny and said it again. He opened the door, telling her you can't sleep in there. Then he knelt down and came back out with a cracker in his hand.

I could see on his face he suspected something happened, but Bailey wasn't talking, and I told him she must have shoved the cracker under the door during the day. He's not a dumb man, but he left it alone.

So far, Bailey read where her mother tried to kill her, wanted her to swallow shards of glass, and locked her in a closet all day.

She knew her mother didn't love her, but this was worse than she thought. Nothing more had happened since as far as she could remember. Probably because once she learned to talk, her mother knew she'd go to her father.

Instead, there were subtle jabs, or she was ignored. She was left to fend for herself, and Bailey didn't mind. She was more than capable of handling her daily duties.

She couldn't let it go though. Her mother needed to suffer for the things she'd done. Bailey wasn't going to let her think she got away with everything all this time.

Her day would come.

***

The normal sparring and snarky jabs continued for several months. Then something terrible happened.

Bailey came through the front door after school to find both of her parents at the kitchen table. Her father spoke first.

"Hey, kiddo. Come sit here at the table, we've got something to tell you."

She looked from his face to her mother's. She had an expression Bailey couldn't remember ever seeing.

Happiness.

"What's going on?" she asked, dropping her bag beside a chair and sitting down.

"Well, honey, it's great news. You're going to be a big sister!" Her father didn't waste any time dropping the bomb.

Bailey's head jerked toward her mother

so fast, her neck popped. "You're pregnant?"

"I am." Her mother nodded.

"You're happy about that?"

Bailey's father touched her arm. "Honey, of course we're happy. Why wouldn't we be? Another baby is a wonderful thing."

She couldn't take her eyes off her mother's. "Is it?"

The two of them stared into each other's eyes, and her mother nodded. "It's a very good thing. I'm very happy about this baby."

This baby. Bailey would have bet all of her books her mother placed emphasis on *this*. As in, *I'm happy about this one, but not the last one.* She looked at her father, hoping to see him pick up on the same thought. He didn't.

"What do you think, Bay? Are *you* happy?"

Bailey stood and gathered her backpack. She looked from her mother to her father and drew out her words, loud and clear.

"No. I am very *not* happy."

She ran up the stairs, into her room, and slammed her door.

***

There were several ways to deal with this situation. She could let it all happen and see if she liked the kid. Maybe they'd get along, and Bailey could teach the little one how to hate their mother. By the time the kid was old enough to understand, Bailey would be almost old enough to leave home. She'd get away from her mother, but her mother would be left with a kind of secondhand Bailey. That would be the best revenge.

But it would take too long.

She could shove her mother down the stairs. Maybe the baby would be aborted *and* her mother would die, laying at the bottom of the steps with a broken neck. A sort of two-for-one.

Or she could break apart some of her mother's pills and stir them into her wine glass. If she used the right ones, they'd make her sleepy, and then maybe they'd burn her insides and her mouth would foam, maybe it would sputter out of her nostrils and Bailey could watch her choke—

"I knew she'd hate it." Bailey heard her mother's voice float up the stairs. She headed to the steps and listened to her parents.

"She'll adjust," her father said. "She's a good kid, and she'll be a good big sister. I don't think we need to worry."

Her mother wasn't buying it.

"Didn't you hear the ice in her voice? 'I am very *not* happy about this.' It didn't sound like a whiny kid who's afraid they'll lose attention. It sounded like she hates this child already."

"Bailey doesn't hate anyone," her father said. She loved the way he always defended her, even when he was wrong. He was her only ally.

"She hates me," her mother said.

"She does not. You two butt heads a lot, yeah. But you make it hard for her too. We were young when we had her, and maybe you weren't quite ready yet. You have some resentments, I think, but I keep hoping they'll work themselves out as she gets older."

Fat chance of that.

"Fat chance of that happening," her mother

said. It was all Bailey could do not to burst into laughter. At least they both understood the future of their relationship. "It's only going to get worse."

"Well, maybe a new baby will help. Maybe it will give her something to focus on other than the tension between the two of you. Maybe it'll help you lay off the wine, too. You'll have to get your shit together. You're not going to make the same mistakes with this one that you made with Bailey. Maybe having another one will bring you closer to Bailey."

Maybe not.

***

It turned out trying to kill someone wasn't as easy as she hoped it would be. First, you had to do it when you wouldn't get caught. When it was only you and your mother in the house all day, it would be easy to figure out who the suspect was once the victim was dead.

Bailey tried.

She left her backpack at the top of the steps, hidden around the corner her mother had to turn to head down in the mornings. Bailey left the arm holes open as much as she could, in the hopes her mother would snag her ankle in them and go flying down the steps. It turned out to be the morning her mother would go into Bailey's room first to grab the laundry on her way down. She saw the backpack on her way out.

"Get your backpack off the stairs," her mother said before she slammed the door.

Mission failed.

Bailey tried crushing some of her mom's medication and adding it to her morning coffee. She thought coffee was a no-go for pregnant people, but her mother didn't seem to care. She sat at the kitchen table eating her cereal before school, and watched her mother take a sip of the coffee, along with a bite of her morning muffin.

Her mother didn't even swallow before she jumped up and ran to the sink, where she spit everything out. She dumped the cup of coffee and dropped the muffin in the trash.

"Goddamned morning sickness."

Another mission failed.

The baby showed up anyway, like she knew it would. Bailey sat in the waiting room with one of her books. She was not the least bit interested in the thing. Her father, on the other hand, was and forced her into the hospital room once her mother and the new baby were settled.

"Bailey, we'd like you to meet your little sister, Annie."

Little sister. Oh great. If she *had* to have a sibling, she hoped for a boy who wouldn't be interested in anything she did. In all her books, the little sister always followed the big sister around and wanted to be just like her.

Ugh.

"Why does it have stuff in its eyes?" she asked, wrinkling her nose in disgust.

"Bailey, her name is Annie. She is not an *it*," her mother snapped. Bailey stared at her, seeing the dark circles under her red, watery eyes. Sometimes her eyes looked like that after she'd had too much to drink, but this time Bailey supposed it was the whole process of forcing a human out of your body.

A week or so before the kid got here, Bailey looked up birthing videos on the internet. Tiny humans came out of a place Bailey had no idea could stretch that way. Once in a while, a baby came out wrong and ripped the mother wide open. Once, she saw a doctor *intentionally* cut a woman with a pair of scissors!

Bailey would never know that feeling because she never, ever, wanted a kid.

She did have to admit the blood was fascinating. After the babies came, it flowed like a river. There was other stuff in it, and sometimes it was chunky, but to her, the crimson liquid was mesmerizing.

"That stuff in her eyes is ointment. It keeps them from getting any infections after she's born," her father interjected, trying to avoid any more tension.

He was good at that. He rescued Bailey from her mother as often as he could. She loved him for it. They were a team.

Bailey stared at the bundle. She was unimpressed. "She's ugly. She looks like one of those flat-faced dogs that snort all the time."

"Bailey, that's very ru—" Before her mother could finish talking, the baby belched, and a white waterfall cascaded from her mouth. The smell was awful. Sour. *Gross.*

"Lenny!"

Her father moved in beside Bailey and took Annie. "I got her."

He always did everything. She saw her mother walk from the bed to the bathroom not long after she came in, so she knew her legs worked. *Why doesn't she get up and clean the kid and change the clothes herself?*

She did not ask for a little sister, and she wasn't consulted prior to the thing being made. She was old enough to know whether she wanted this or not and to be a part of family decisions. Had anyone bothered to ask her, she would have said no.

No way, José. No way.

***

Bailey tried her best to avoid her little sister at all costs. For the most part it worked, until Annie got old enough for her mother to pawn her off on Bailey while she drank and watched her soap operas.

There was a list of things Bailey was not allowed to do with the baby. She was not allowed to bathe or burp her, or put her down to sleep. Everything else was fair game. Diapers, puke, and snot were daily occurrences in Bailey's life these days.

One afternoon, her mother came down the stairs dressed in a white sundress with bright yellow daisies. She was wearing full makeup, and her hair was up in a perfect high ponytail.

Just like the one that hangs over a horse's butt.

No yoga pants, no messy bun, and makeup. This meant she was headed next door to see Mrs. Klein. Her mother always had to look perfect when she was around the neighbors. She even took fresh baked cookies—that she baked *herself!*—next door sometimes.

The family never got any fresh baked anything. But to Mrs. Klein, Janet Heron was the perfect mother, the perfect wife, and the perfect neighbor.

"I don't want to watch her. I just want to read in my room."

"I could really use a break, Bay," her mother said. "Just some time to do Mom things."

"Fine." Nobody asked Bailey if *she* needed time to do *Bailey* things.

Three hours later, Annie woke up yelling. Her mother still wasn't home. She ran down her mental checklist. Diaper? Clean. Hot? No. Cold? Also, no.

"Hungry?" Bailey asked. Annie answered with more yelling, escalating to screams.

It wasn't on Bailey's get-a-grown-up list, but she had never fed Annie before. She saw her mother do it a million times. The bottles for the day were already mixed and waiting in the refrigerator. She would heat one up and give it to Annie. Easy.

She grabbed a bottle, shook it, and put it in the microwave, hesitating. Her mom didn't usually put them in here, but Bailey wasn't allowed to use the stove to boil water like her mom did before. What was the difference? Both ways would heat the formula. How long should she put it in for? One minute? Two?

It was pretty cold, so it would need a while, probably. She tapped the numbers and set it for two minutes. One didn't seem like enough.

When the microwave beeped, Bailey reached for the bottle. The plastic was hot, but not too hot to hold. She took it over to Annie, shook it again, and shoved the nipple into Annie's mouth.

The baby suckled for a second and then tossed her head from side to side, knocking the nipple out and beating the air with her tiny fists. Bailey let go, and the bottle fell to the floor. Annie's screams were louder than ever.

The back door flew open, and her mother came running in, dropping to her knees over Annie. "What's wrong with her? What did you do?" She looked at Bailey, eyes blazing with anger.

"She was hungry. I tried to feed her," Bailey answered.

Her mom grabbed the bottle. She squeezed a couple drops onto her wrist. Hissing, she yanked it back.

"Bailey! That's too hot! How did you heat it?"

Bailey stared at the carpet. She couldn't help but feel glad her sister was hurting. She knew it wasn't right, to enjoy someone's pain—but it felt so *good*.

"A couple of minutes in the microwave."

Her mother cradled Annie, kissing her face and wiping tears from her cheeks. Bailey had a flash memory of falling off her bike in the driveway as a little girl. Her knee was bleeding, and her wrist hurt. Her mother came out and told her to be careful she didn't scratch the car when she lifted the bike back up.

There were no kisses or tear drying for Bailey.

"A couple? Two minutes? In the microwave? Are you serious?"

Bailey nodded.

"You don't stick a bottle in the microwave for two minutes! You have to do it little by little! I do it fifteen to thirty seconds at a time, Bailey." She couldn't remember the last time she saw her mother this angry. This ... protective. "And you test it first! You could have blistered her throat! What the fuck is wrong with you!"

"Well *SORRRRRY*," she yelled. Bailey's world went into slow-motion. Everything was muffled, as if someone stuck cotton in her ears. "I didn't *know* I wasn't supposed to feed her! If you were home, *you* could have done it! But *no*, you go over to Mrs. Klein's like you do *every day*!" She was surprised to find herself this upset. She never raised her voice to her mom, not like this. Sure, she cried and got loud, but never like this.

Her mother held Annie, both of them goggling at her. One of her hands was over Annie's midsection in a protective hold. She chewed her lip, staring at her daughter. Bailey could almost smell the fear radiating off of her. *Good*.

"I don't even *like* her! I never even *wanted* her!" She bent down and picked up the bottle and hurled it at the wall. Two framed photos of Annie fell to the floor, and Bailey stomped on one, creating a spider's web of glass over her sister's frozen face.

That's an improvement.

She looked at her mother and spoke, slow and loud.

"I wish she were dead."

The slap produced a crack that bounced off the walls. Bailey fell backward, biting her lower lip as her rear hit the floor. She tasted blood, like when she busted her lip last summer after slipping at the creek.

Everything was back to normal speed, and she could hear clearly again.

The three of them froze, Annie with her thumb in her mouth and eyes wide. Finally,

25

her mother spoke. "Bailey Marie, Annie is your sister. She is not going anywhere. You *will* learn to love her. Now go upstairs."

Bailey crossed her arms and gritted her teeth.

"Right. Fucking. Now. Get upstairs!"

She took off up the steps, running as fast as she could. *I will not learn to love her.* She had no idea what the consequences for such an outburst would be. She was pretty sure she could convince her father she meant well. Annie was hungry, and she tried to feed her when Mom wasn't around.

He would see. Bailey didn't *mean* to hurt her. But she didn't feel bad about it either. She wasn't even sorry.

Accidents happen.

***

Sitting on her perch, Bailey listened.

"She did what?" her father asked.

"Your daughter overheated a bottle and fed Annie with it."

"Is Annie okay?" Concern. It was expected. He loved Annie, even if Bailey was his favorite. She tolerated it.

"Look for yourself."

"She looks fine to me."

"Open her mouth and look at her tongue. There's a blister forming in the back!"

Bailey snuck a peek around the corner and saw her father lift Annie from her playpen. He pulled her lower lip down with his finger and looked in her mouth.

"I don't see a blister. Her mouth looks

fine. And she's smiling. No harm done."

"No harm done? *No harm done?*"

"It was an accident, Jan."

Yes it was.

"You should know better than to leave them home alone. I've told you time and again something bad could happen. You're lucky it wasn't something worse."

Bailey heard that familiar clink.

"Sure, put it on me. Your *prodigy* child almost burned our baby from the inside out, but you're right, it's my fault."

Really, Mom?

Her dad was laughing. "Oh, come on. Could you be any more dramatic? 'Almost burned our baby from the inside out.' That's insane. The formula was a little hot. Annie's fine. I'll tell her not to feed the baby again, and it'll all be over."

"That's not all she did."

"Okay? What did you leave out?"

"When I got on to her about feeding the baby, she lost it, Lenny. I mean she just lost it."

Bailey heard her father walking to the kitchen and smelled fresh ground coffee in the air. She loved that smell. It always reminded her of him when he wasn't around.

"She cried? She felt bad about what happened. I'm not surprised she had a fit."

"This wasn't a fit. And she didn't cry. She yelled at me. She's never done that before. She lost all of her composure."

"Why was she yelling at you?"

There was a long pause. Bailey knew why her mother was hesitant.

"She said I should have been here to feed her."

Winner, winner, chicken dinner.

"She's not wrong."

"Again, take her side. Anyway, she grabbed the bottle and threw it across the room at the wall. It knocked two of Annie's photos off the wall. She stomped on Annie's face." Bailey heard her mother open a drawer and fish something out of it. "Look at this."

She heard her father snort.

"So, she 'stomped on Annie's face?' Really, Jan? You and your damned dramatics. She stepped on a photo. She was mad, and she let it out. It's not a good way to do it, I'll give you that, but don't you think you're reading a bit too much into this?"

"She told me she didn't like her sister and never wanted her."

"Janet, relax. She's having a little trouble adjusting. I'll talk to her. She won't do it again. Cut the kid some slack."

Bailey stood and made it back to her bed without making a sound. She heard her father's footsteps trailing after her. She dove under the covers, turned on her lamp, and opened a book.

"Knock, knock."

This won't be so bad. He was down there defending you. Play this right, and everything will be fine.

"Come in," she said.

He came in and dragged her chair from her desk to her bed, turning it around the wrong way and straddling it. "Hey, kid. Whatcha reading?"

She slid her bookmark into place and showed him the cover: *Killer Klowns.*

"Well, your teacher ought to be impressed

with that." He shook his head and chuckled.

Bailey giggled and rolled her eyes.

"So, Mom tells me something happened today."

She nodded. "Yeah. It was an accident, Dad. I didn't mean to burn her. I thought I was helping, and Mom wasn't here."

"I know, Bay. You were trying, and you made a mistake. It could have hurt her."

Show time. She conjured up a tear and let it trail down her cheek. She followed it with a sniffle. "I know. And I'm so sorry. I wouldn't have done it if I knew it could hurt her. Is she okay?"

Her father took her hand. *It's working.*

"Oh, honey, she's fine." He wiped her tear away with his finger. "Just next time she's hungry, I think you should go get Mom, okay? She'll come do it. I don't think she's going to Mrs. Klein's for a while now, so she will be here to take care of everything."

"Yes, sir. That sounds good." *Blah blah blah.*

"Now, we have another little problem to talk about." He looked serious, but the corners of his mouth were turned up, so she knew it couldn't be that bad.

"You got really angry, Bay, and I understand that. You were probably scared, and probably felt really bad about Annie." He looked to her for confirmation.

She nodded and allowed a few more tears and a fresh sniffle.

"You can't act out like that, honey. You can't throw things. And you can't smash glass with your foot. You could have cut yourself. Mommy was very scared and worried about you."

She wasn't worried about me. She was worried

about her baby. But you're right on the scared part. I scared her pretty good.

She looked down at her bed in an effort to hide a grin trying to sneak its way onto her face.

"I know. I'm sorry. I won't do it again."

"I know. I know you're having a hard time with the baby. You probably feel like we don't pay attention to you, and I'm not gonna pretend we're perfect. I have to work, and your mother … well, she struggles too. But give it some time. Be patient with everyone." He rose from the chair and leaned down over her.

"Yes, sir." Bailey nodded.

He kissed her forehead. "All right, get to sleep. No more *Killer Klowns*. Tomorrow's a new day."

***

After the feeding fiasco, Bailey kept her distance from Annie and her mother. There hadn't been anymore outbursts from either side. Bailey spoke to her mother when spoken to and ignored the existence of her little sister.

Until she couldn't.

One morning, she opened her bedroom door to find Annie sitting on the floor. Her books were in a messy pile instead of in the bookcase where they belonged. Several had their covers torn off. Scattered around Annie were loose pages ripped from their worlds.

And slobber. All over the books, the pages, everywhere. Like some rabid, foam-faced dog had the wrong idea about alphabet soup. She had a book in her mouth, chewing on it the way a rat would chew on a cracker box.

The odd slow-motion feeling came over Bailey again. Invisible hands slipped ear muffs over her ears. Another pair strapped lead weights to her wrists and ankles.

It took her a long time to build her collection. The library next to her school sometimes threw books out by the dumpster when they were old, but sometimes even when they looked brand new! She had no idea why people who worked in a library, who were supposed to love books, could throw them out along with old salad and coffee grounds. Why not donate them somewhere? Worlds and characters, things that lived and breathed in her mind, tossed into the trash.

It made her cry.

She often rescued the books and brought them home. The school wouldn't allow her to check out anything other than baby books. She didn't earn an allowance. Once in a while, her father would bring her a book or let her buy one on a rare trip out together. She collected them three or four at a time from the public library on her way home from school.

And now here was Annie, destroying them. Bailey snatched away the book she was chewing on. The spine split Annie's lip, and blood and saliva mixed before spilling over her lip and down her chin in red rivers.

"Don't you EVER come in here again!" The distorted sound in her head made her sound quieter than she was, so she yelled even louder. "You ruined my books!" She made herself as big and scary as she could, feeling spit leave her lips with every word. Her face felt hot enough to set the pages scattered around her on fire.

"You're not allowed in my room, you little brat!" She was shoving Annie toward the door when her mother appeared.

"What's going on in here? Why are you screaming at her?"

"She came in my room and ruined my books! Look at them!" She picked one up and stroked its spine, tears falling down her cheeks.

"She doesn't know any better, Bailey. It was an accident."

"It's not an accident! She did it on purpose!" Bailey snapped.

Her mother knelt and lifted Annie up, resting her on her hip. She bounced up and down, and Annie slowly caught her breath and stopped crying.

"It's an accident when she doesn't know what she's doing. I swear you love those books more than you do any of us," her mother said. She turned her head to kiss Annie's cheek and stopped.

"Why is her lip bleeding?" Her mother raked her thumb over Annie's lip, smearing the blood onto her cheek.

The color blood looks good on her, Bailey thought. She looked at the blood on her mother's thumb. *On both of them, actually.*

"She was chewing on my book, and I took it away from her."

"Took it away how?"

"I yanked it out of her mouth. I was trying to save my book. I didn't mean for her to bite her lip. It was an *accident.*" Bailey did not try to hide her grin.

Her mother's eyes widened, and she took a step back, avoiding Bailey's eyes. It was fun, catching her off guard. She turned and left the room, leaving Bailey to collect her wet, torn books from the floor. She knew deep down the books were ruined now, but she couldn't bear to throw them away. Instead, she stacked them in a neat pile near her bed.

She *did* love her books—more than any human on the planet. She even loved them a little more than she loved her dad. They took her to places far, far away, and the characters in them were better than any real person she knew.

Bailey didn't have any friends. She tried a few times over the years, but she was different from the other kids.

In the second grade, there was Melanie. Bailey met her in the library. She sat down beside her and tossed her backpack onto the table. Melanie was reading one of the Amelia Bedelia books. *Those books are for babies* was her first thought. But then she decided someone who liked to read might be cool to hang out with. They wouldn't be trading books or anything, but maybe they could talk about them anyway.

"Hi." Melanie closed her book.

"Hey."

"What's your name?"

Bailey introduced herself. So far so good.

"You like to read?" Melanie asked.

"Yeah. I read a lot," Bailey answered.

"Me, too. What kind of stuff do you like to read?"

Bailey pulled her book out of her backpack and showed Melanie the cover.

"*Scary Stories to Tell in the Dark*," Melanie read aloud. "Yikes. What's that about?"

Bailey shrugged. "Ghosts and monsters and stuff like that."

"That's gross. You like that stuff?"

Bailey felt her face flush. "Yeah, so?"

"You're weird." Melanie gathered her things and walked away from the table.

She tried again once in a while, when she saw someone with potential. It never worked. Bailey liked different things than most kids her age. She wasn't into dresses or boys or anything the other girls liked. She didn't eat lunch with anyone or go to functions or participate in any clubs. She carried her backpack of books, found quiet places to sit, and dove into the worlds splayed on the pages. Most of the time, she liked it that way.

But once in a while, she wished deep down for a friend. Just one.

***

The old oak tree in the front yard was her favorite reading spot, but it was too easy for her mother to come and bother her. A small creek ran behind the house, and Bailey took to reading there instead. She liked the quiet splashing sounds the water made as it flowed through the rocks.

Settling down on a dry spot, she opened her book. She'd finished *Killer Klowns* and moved on to a story about a car that was possessed and murdered people.

A soft whimper floated across the creek. Bailey looked out toward the noise and saw a dog. He wasn't very big and didn't look like any particular breed. He lowered his front legs level with the ground, his butt in the air, tail wagging fast; he yipped at her.

"Hey, puppy," she said. "What are you doing out here?"

His whole body wiggled, still lowered and ready to pounce.

"Come here, boy." She patted the ground beside her.

It was all the invitation he needed. He crossed the creek, bowled her over, and covered her in kisses. He was soaking wet after his dip in the creek. She ran her hands down his back, smoothing his wet fur, and scratched his cheeks. He continued to smother her in puppy breath.

Once introductions were over, he settled in beside her, rested his head on her knee, and looked up at her.

"Do you have a home?"

The dog did not answer.

"You look pretty skinny, and you don't have a collar. I guess you're probably a stray." It was obvious nobody cared for him. He was kind of like her, on his own with nobody to watch out for him. Well, she had her dad, at least, but he didn't count because he wasn't around much anymore. This little guy didn't have anybody. She was surprised he was still friendly. It wasn't easy being nice when people treated you bad.

"You need a name." She looked him over. "In one of my books, this boy has a dog named Barkley. I always liked it, and he was a really good dog. He was really smart, and they did everything together. Do you like that name?"

The dog playfully gnawed on her fingers. He seemed fine with it.

"Barkley."

He barked and jumped onto her lap. She laughed and jumped up, running around the yard while he chased her. Once in a while, she slowed down enough for him to catch her, and they rolled in the grass, play-fighting. It was the first time she felt happy in as long as she could remember.

"You must be hungry. There's food at the house, but ..." Bailey's eyes dropped, and she frowned. She hadn't thought this far ahead.

Barkley tilted his head, looking up at her, as if to say, *but what?*

"I don't know if my mom and dad will let me keep you. I don't want them to call the pound. Maybe I should just hide you."

It sounded like a good idea, but it wouldn't work. She was pretty sure she'd get caught. For sure, her mother would make her give him up. It was better to tell now and ask permission. Maybe she could convince her dad, and he could work on her mom.

She dropped down to her knees and put her forehead against the pup's. She looked him straight in the eyes.

"I just found you, and I already know you'll be better than any little sister," she said.

***

"No way."

Dinner was already on the table, and her mother was wiping down counters with a dishtowel. Barkley sat outside, watching the conversation through the back screened door.

"I already have to pick up after you and your sister. I'm not cleaning up after a dog."

"I'll do everything, Momma," Bailey promised. She was trying her best to play the innocent, sweet child. Something about the word *Momma* sounded sweeter. It sounded like *Oh please, Momma, I'm just a child who wants a dog. I'll be a very good girl from now on, I swear!* But of course, Bailey knew better.

"I'll feed him and wash him and potty train him." Dogs were better than kids. There were no nasty diapers, and you could just wash them outside with a garden hose. *You should try it with Annie, Momma.*

"No, Bailey."

At just the right time, her father walked in the front door from work. Bailey ran to him and hugged him tight.

"Dad! I found a dog! He's so cute! I named him Barkley! I really want to keep him, but Mom says no. He's a great dog, and I can teach him everything. I'll—"

"Whoa, kiddo, slow down," he laughed. He headed into the kitchen and kissed her mother on the cheek.

Yuck.

"What's this about a dog?"

Her mother turned around and leaned against the counter. "Your daughter found a dog at the creek today."

Bark! Bailey translated him in her head: *that's me!*

"Well look at you," her father said, leaning down and pressing his hand against the screen. Barkley tried to lick it. "He's pretty cute, isn't he?"

"No."

"Oh, come on. He seems friendly. He's

young so he'll be easy to train. Let the kid have the dog. I'll help her out."

It felt good, having her father defend her. Her mom wasn't very nice to him either, it seemed, so they had that in common. He was always nice to her and asked her how her day went and checked on her every night before bed. He wasn't perfect, but he was close.

"You're not home enough to 'help her out.' He'll shit in the floor in the middle of the day, and I'll be the one cleaning it up while Bailey's at school. No."

"I'll leave him outside while I'm gone," Bailey said.

"And when he chews up everything in the house? When he destroys your favorite slippers? When he topples over a vase?"

Yeah, Dad, if he topples over a vase, she might let him eat the pieces so he'll die, and she won't have to deal with him anymore.

"We'll just be more careful. She'll only bring him in at night, to sleep. Let her have that much. He'll stay in her room and her room only, right, Bay?" She could see her hope reflected in his eyes. He already loved Barkley too.

"Yes, I promise. He won't be in the house."

Her mother looked long and hard at her father, her hand on her hip and her lips pressed together.

"Sure, I'm always the bad cop, and you're mister perfect."

She saw her father roll his eyes ever so slightly.

"Fine. If you guys want the dog, it's your dog. I won't feed it, bathe it, or clean up after it. If it shits on the floor, it'll stay there until one of you cleans it up."

Oh sure, like you're going to let your precious Annie crawl around in dog crap.

"His name is *Barkley*. He is not an *it*," Bailey said.

She waited. Finally, her mother's eyes widened, then narrowed. *Ha! Whatcha got to say to that one? I win!*

Bailey watched her mother wind the dishtowel around her hand until her fingers turned purple. "Fine. Barkley. He is yours, so he is your problem. He does not go in Annie's room or mess with any of her toys. And do *not* let him lick her!"

Her father opened the screen door. "Welcome home, boy!"

Barkley ran inside. He pounced on Bailey and moved on to her father, sucking up all the new smells of the people and the house. Next, he headed for the couch, sprung off the ground and onto the white, flower-patterned cushions, leaving muddy paw prints in his wake. Her mother followed, screeching. She whipped the dishtowel at his behind.

"Goddamned dog!" she yelled. "You better catch him before I do, or he's fucking dead!"

Barkley headed for the table and up onto a dining chair. He snatched a chunk of the ham her mother had been slow baking all day.

Her father opened the back door, and Bailey led Barkley onto the porch. "Stay here, boy, and I'll come get you for bed," she said, scratching his head. "That was a dumb idea, stealing dinner like that. You can't stay if you keep that up." She hoped he understood.

Later that night, she brought Barkley up

to bed with her. He snuggled up close and kept her warm.

Best friend ever.

***

"I don't want a birthday party."

"I don't care, you're having one," her mother said.

Bailey stood by the door with her arms crossed over her chest. She knew the only reason her mother wanted this party was so she could look good in front of the other parents, the same way she did with Mrs. Klein. The PTA mothers and fathers would drop their kids off, and Bailey's mom would be standing in the doorway, smiling. She would expect Bailey to greet everyone and say thank you. Bailey had to be the perfect child so her mother could look perfect.

Nothing was ever about Bailey when it came to her mother.

"I don't even know the kids in my class. I barely even talk to them."

"That's because all you do is carry around your books and shut everybody out. We'll invite the whole class, and you can leave your books in your room and actually socialize. It's not healthy for you to ignore everybody."

Bailey rolled her eyes. *Like you care what's healthy for me.*

"Do we have to invite the whole class? Can I just invite a few kids?"

"No, not just a few." Her mother mirrored her stance and crossed her arms over her own chest. "The entire class. You don't want kids feeling left out."

She was fuming inside. She didn't care if kids felt left out. Her mother had no idea how her days at school went, or who she did or didn't talk to. No, she didn't have any friends. But she didn't care. Most of them left her alone—except for one.

Leo.

"I *don't* want a party."

"Well, I don't care what you want."

"You never do."

Her mother knelt down in front of her and cupped her chin, squeezing tight. It was her go-to move, keeping Bailey from turning away from her so she could chastise her. Bailey was unafraid and stared into her mother's eyes.

"You will take these invitations to school, and you will hand out every single one. To *all* the kids in your class. If I find out you missed *anyone*," she squeezed harder, "you'll be made to apologize in front of the whole class. Do you understand me?"

She knew Bailey would *never* want to stand in front of a room full of people. Bailey *hated* people. Since she'd found Barkley, those feelings only became stronger. People were horrible. Well, except her dad, but even he was a mess sometimes.

Bailey locked eyes with her mother. "I am not inviting Leo."

"Who's Leo?" Her mother let go.

"He's a boy in my class. He's mean, and I don't want him at my house."

"This isn't *your* house, it's mine and your father's. Last I checked, you didn't pay any rent or bills."

Bailey fought hard not to roll her eyes.

"What do you mean he's mean? What does he do?"

Why are you even asking? You don't care! Maybe her mom was glad someone was being mean to her.

"He calls me names. And once, he pushed me." She wasn't expecting any sympathy, and she was rewarded with exactly that.

"So, if he pushes you again, push him back," she said. "Kids are mean. That's life, honey." *Honey* dripped off her lips and reminded Bailey of old women who waitressed in truck stops in the movies she'd seen on TV. They wore too much makeup and always had a cigarette in their hand, usually carrying a coffee pot along with it.

"You will invite him to the party. Maybe you two can talk and be friends."

Bailey raised her voice. She knew her dad asked her not to, but she didn't care. She was getting dizzy and had a touch of the slow-motion feeling again. She slid her arms through the loopholes on her backpack, pulling it on. "I don't want him here!"

Bailey took a backhand to the face. It wasn't the first time and wouldn't be the last, she was sure. She did not flinch or cry. Her lips turned up in a smile, and she leaned a hair forward, as if asking for another. She locked her eyes onto her mother's.

The slight movement Bailey made sent her mother back two steps, her eyes widening. Her lips parted, and Bailey heard her take in a sharp breath.

I win.

Her mother was afraid of her. It made her feel warm inside, like sipping a hot bowl of soup on a snowy day.

It didn't last long.

Her chin was once again cupped and squeezed. "Listen here, young lady. You are *done* talking to me like this! You will *not* yell at me again! This boy is coming to your party. I don't care what you want."

Big surprise.

Bailey bit her bottom lip, hard. She held her hands in front of her to keep from lunging. In her mind, she pounced. She imagined herself scratching her mother's eyes until they bled. Then she could see herself biting meaty chunks out of her cheek and spitting blood in her face. Her mother would scream and fall, and Bailey would climb on top of her. She'd pull her mother's hair so hard her scalp would tear. Then she'd wrap her hands around her mother's throat—

She was forced back into reality when her mother crammed the invitations into her backpack. She shoved her out the door.

One of these days ... Bailey thought. *One of these days.*

***

When she got to school, she placed an envelope at every kid's desk. The last one was for Leo. She contemplated throwing it away, or spilling something on it, but the threat of having to apologize to Leo in front of the class was worse than inviting him. He probably wouldn't come anyway.

When Leo showed up and saw the envelope, he smiled at her from across the room.

Oh great. He'll be worse than ever. He better not think I like him, she thought. A shiver ran down her body, and she wanted to throw up.

When the teacher dismissed them for their first break, Bailey headed outside with her book. The playground was large, with jungle gyms and monkey bars. There were hopscotch grids drawn on the concrete, and over to the side were several picnic benches. This was where Bailey read her books every day.

As she opened her book and began to read, a walrus-shaped shadow fell over her. She looked up, and Leo threw the envelope at her face. He was a big kid, twice her size. All he ever brought in his lunch box was leftover pizza or fast food and a soda.

"So, you're having a party, huh?"

"Yeah, but you don't have to go."

He laughed. "Oh, yeah I do. I want to see what kind of shithole you live in."

"Nice vocabulary," she said. Her body was stiff, and she clenched her teeth until she felt throbbing in her jaw. *Take it easy.* "Is this your second or third year of fifth grade?"

Leo's face went dark, but he said nothing. *Good. Keep your fat mouth shut.*

"I don't live in a hole," she said. She'd never said a swear word in her life and wasn't about to start.

"I didn't say *hole*, dumbass. I said *shithole*. Because you smell like shit. So, your house must be made of shit." Bailey thought he'd fall over laughing and wasn't sure how he would ever get

44

up again if he did.

He really needs to work on his insults, she thought. There were books out there that could teach him, but Leo probably couldn't read anyway.

She stood up to leave, chuckling at the voice inside her head. When she rounded the corner of the bench, Leo stepped in front of her. He smelled like onions and sweat. For the second time that day, she thought she might be sick.

He shoved her back down on the bench. Her book fell to the concrete, and he stood on top of it. It was a book about child wizards. She had a report due next week, and the teacher didn't approve of her typical reading material. She kind of liked it, but she wouldn't admit that to anyone.

The spine crushed under his weight, and she could almost hear the characters screaming for help. *Get off me, bugger! Sod off!* She wished they could cast spells up at him and send him flying into the sky. The thought of Leo launching into the air and casting a massive shadow on the playground made her giggle.

"Don't laugh at me, you little bitch," he said.

"Just give me my book, and leave me alone."

He spat at her, a large, gelatinous chunk landing on her chin and sliding off, falling to the concrete with a *splat.*

Something inside her snapped. She felt it go. Walls she built around herself crumbled; all safety locks on her brain broke open. Her heart beat in a rhythm she never felt before. All restraint was gone.

So, if he pushes you again, push him back.

For once in her life, Bailey took her mother's advice. She shoved Leo with everything inside her.

Leo wasn't expecting it. He went after her all this time because she never fought back. He usually got bored after a minute or two because she didn't talk back and left her alone, but this time, she'd laughed at him. He fell backward, arms splayed out in an attempt to catch himself.

He missed.

He landed flat on his back, and his head bounced off the ground. It reminded her of the time her father dropped a cantaloupe in the driveway. It was a kind of *crack, splish* sound. The noise sent little bolts of electricity through her body. The hair on her arms stood up, and she couldn't stand still.

Her stomach had a funny feeling too—an odd sense of hunger.

She stood over Leo, breathing shallow and fast. He wasn't moving. The world around her went silent again, and she had the now familiar slow-motion feeling. It was like watching a movie with the sound turned off. She could see the pool of blood spreading around Leo's head.

Bailey stood fascinated as she watched his body jerk and his head move from side to side. Small, foamy bubbles rose from between his lips, like the bubbles that rose in a pot when her daddy boiled eggs in the mornings.

You're supposed to roll him on his side so he doesn't choke on his tongue or vomit, she remembered reading in a book. Instead, she watched the blood spread to her sneakers, and the white trim around the sole turned crimson.

She made mental notes of everything happening with Leo's body. She couldn't look away and watched the whites of his eyes as his eyelids fluttered open and closed. She watched the cords in his neck tighten. Blood seeped from his nostrils and mouth, and a slow trickle came from his ears.

He stopped seizing and lay motionless. Bailey watched as his chest rose ... and then he deflated like a balloon. *Ha!* It made her so happy to know he wouldn't be there to bother her anymore. A weight rose from her shoulders, and she felt light and giddy.

She started laughing.

Noooo! Stop laughing! She laughed harder. *They're gonna think I'm crazy.* Tears ran down her face, and she clutched her belly.

She looked up and saw the teacher on duty, her mouth open in what could have been a harrowing scream or a yawn. *Or maybe she's laughing with me!* She couldn't hear, but she guessed that was not the right answer.

Mrs. Jaharty grabbed her by the shoulders, and the sound returned to Bailey's ears. She'd been laughing so hard she had the hiccups.

And that made her laugh even harder.

She was taken to the edge of the playground while the other students were escorted back inside. An ambulance was called, and Leo was taken off the playground on a stretcher. She hadn't seen him move since the seizure, and they had him hooked up to tubes. Someone was on top of him, doing CPR.

Wasting your time, guys. He's dead as dead gets. Like, maggots-are-gonna-eat-him dead.

Decomposing. No sign of intelligent life. There wasn't any when he was alive either!

The laughing finally stopped when a policeman walked over to ask her questions. She recounted the events: he came to her, he said mean things, she tried to leave, he pushed and spat, she pushed back. The policeman told her again and again it wasn't her fault. "Whatever happens, don't blame yourself, okay?" She stiffened when he hugged her, and he gave her a stuffed bear from his patrol car's trunk.

She knew she should feel bad, but she didn't. She wasn't sorry or sad. He was dead, and just like that, her life was better. The only thing she was sorry about was her shoes. She only wore them a week.

What a shame.

***

She was already awake and looking forward to a Leo-less day at school when her father called her down for breakfast.

What's he doing home? He was usually long gone by this time. She dressed and gathered her backpack, then headed downstairs. When she reached the dining room, she found both of her parents sitting side by side. They never sat that way.

Something is definitely up.

"Hey, honey, good morning," her father said. Bailey sat down in the chair across from him. She glanced at her mother, who was studying her harder than usual.

"Hey, Dad. What's going on? What are you doing home?"

"I took the day off to spend some time with you."

Does he not know it's a school day? What planet is this? "Dad, it's a school day."

"Not today, it isn't. Your school took the next couple of days off." He flicked his eyes to her mother's and frowned. He took a deep breath and then said: "Honey, your classmate, Leo, he didn't make it."

Duh. I already knew that.

"They were able to bring him back during the ride to the hospital, but he passed away overnight, Bay. I'm so sorry about your friend." He reached across the table and took her hands in his.

My friend? Bailey looked at her mother, who seemed to be studying her reactions. She didn't feel quite as bad about this as her father did. But then, her mother knew Bailey hated Leo.

Have to be careful what I say. She looked down at her father's hands wrapped around hers and mustered up some tears. She was pretty good at that these days. It was a skill that came in handy.

"He died?"

Her father nodded. "He did, honey. His brain—" her father stopped, considering his words. "His brain hemorrhaged. Do you know what that means?"

I didn't even know he had any brains.

"Like, it was bleeding, right?"

For a moment, her father beamed at her before his face went somber again. Bailey swelled with pride, knowing she'd once again impressed her dad. That always made her feel good.

49

"Yes, that's right. He had a brain bleed, and it was too much for him to recover from."

Her mother jumped in. "Bailey, what happened on the playground?" She leaned forward and narrowed her eyes. Bailey figured this was coming.

She looked down at the table and made her voice tiny and quiet. "I told you he was mean to me, Momma."

Her father's head snapped to his right, eyeing her mother. "She told you this kid was a bully?"

Sure did, Dad. But you haven't even heard the best part.

Her mother twisted her fingers. The trap had been laid, and her mother was caught, squirming. "She mentioned it yesterday, when I was giving her the party invitations. She didn't want to invite him, she said he was mean to her. But I thought if they spent some time together outside of school—"

"You were going to force her to be around some boy who's been mean to her?" Her father's voice was loud. "You invited this boy to our house? Why would you make her do that?"

Yeah, Momma, why would you make me do that? Poor me.

"I thought maybe he liked her or something, I don't know. I thought they could be friends. I wanted her to have a nice birthday party."

Oh geez, laying it on thick there, Mom.

Her father looked back in her direction. "How was this boy mean to you? What did he do?"

"Well, he called me names. He called me

the b-word once. And once he pushed me."

Her father's face went red. "He pushed you? Did you tell anyone?"

Ta-da! Finally.

"Well, no, not until yesterday. I told Mom about it when we were talking about the party."

"And what did she say, Bailey?" Her father turned toward her mother again, gritting his teeth.

Her mother's eyes locked onto hers like heat seeking missiles. Bailey smiled, baring every one of her little white teeth. She saw the tiniest bit of a head shake, and her mother's eyes grew two sizes.

Before her father turned his head back to her, Bailey wiped the smile off her face, putting her sad mask back on. "She said if he pushed me again, to push him back."

Her mother went stiff, and Bailey watched her father jump out of his chair so fast, it fell over backward and clattered across the floor. "Bailey, get upstairs. Your mother and I need to talk." He was still gritting his teeth, and she could see his jaw clenching and unclenching.

Gone and done it now, haven't you, Momma? She opened the door to let Barkley in and then ran for the steps. She settled onto her perch, Barkley beside her. This was a show she was *not* going to miss.

"Why the hell wouldn't you tell me our daughter was being bullied?"

"I told you, I thought if he came to the party, they'd learn to get along."

"You were having that party so the other parents wouldn't talk about you, Janet. You don't give a damn about a child's birthday party, so stop pretending."

Great minds think alike!

She heard her mother's chair scrape the floor. "I didn't know it was that bad. He pushed her once. You want her to just take that? You would have told her to push back too!"

There was silence for a moment. And then her father: "I would have taught her to defend herself, but first we should have gone to the boy's parents. I could have talked to them."

"Yeah, and that would have made it all worse."

Hate to admit it, but she's probably right on that one.

Her mother spoke again. "The bigger problem here is that your daughter killed a child."

It didn't happen often, but it happened right then. She heard the slap, her mother's gasp, and her father's grunt all at once.

You deserve it, she thought, and caught herself smiling again.

"So, it's okay for men—boys, I mean—to hit girls," her mother said. There were no tears in her voice, and she sounded strong. Bailey admired that, which was a feeling she hated, but it was only a little bit.

"Oh, Janet, shut the fuck up. You bring me to that point. You battle and you nag and just poke, poke, poke. This kid targeted Bailey when she did nothing wrong. There's a difference. *Our* daughter did *not* kill a child."

"Of course, Bailey did nothing wrong. She never does."

Sarcastic much, Mother?

"The bottom line is he's dead because she

pushed him," her mother said.

"She pushed him because *you* told her to! If she hadn't been forced to invite this kid to her party—oh, I'm sorry, *your* party—he might not have confronted her!" Bailey could feel the anger, like smoke floating through the living room and up the stairs, vibrating her body.

Get her, Dad!

Bailey heard footsteps, and the familiar squeal of the recliner as her father collapsed onto it. "You are a terrible mother."

Amen!

Bailey heard the refrigerator open, the *pop!* of the wine cork and the sound of the bottle neck clinking against a glass. This was her cue to get to her bedroom, because her mother was on her way up to her own.

She closed her door and flopped down on her bed. "Well, Barks, guess the party's canceled." This time she laughed aloud.

Barkley looked up at her and licked her chin. "Serves the bitch right," she said. The curse word felt good on her lips, like sweet strawberry lip balm. She grabbed him and held him tight. For once, she didn't feel so alone. She had Barkley, who was always by her side, and her father always defended her. They were on her side.

That made it three against two.

***

School was different now that Leo was gone. The kids got over Leo's death fast, but they couldn't get over Bailey's role in it. There were other kids he bullied besides Bailey, and once one of them smiled at her in the hallway. He still kept his distance, but it made her feel good about her *accident.*

Then there were the kids who were afraid of her. That was even better. Nobody tried to talk to her. Kids moved their desks a little farther away from hers in class. Anyone she looked at would look away as fast as they could. She dropped a textbook in one of her classes once, and the sound it made when it hit the floor made everyone jump out of their desks and look at her.

Outside on the playground, one kid managed to find the courage to come over to her. She sat on the same bench she did the day Leo died. The kid, Ryan, sat across from her. He dumped out his backpack and started working on homework.

Bailey kept her head down and raised her eyes to his face. It took several seconds for Ryan to realize she was staring. Finally, he looked up at her.

"What?"

She said nothing.

"Stop staring at me, freak."

She forced a growl from deep down in her throat, vibrating her chest. One corner of her mouth rose in a crooked smile.

"Uh, okay." Ryan didn't take his eyes off Bailey as he gathered his things and crammed them into his backpack. She watched one of his pencils roll off the table onto the ground. He didn't notice.

She let him gather everything and walk a few steps away.

"Hey."

Ryan turned and looked over his shoulder. "You dropped a pencil."

He came back to the bench and knelt down to pick it up. As he rose back up, Bailey started growling again. When his face met hers, it was full of fear instead of the judgment it held a few minutes before.

Bailey barked.

Ryan dropped the pencil and took off running for the building and the other kids, not looking back this time.

She couldn't hold it in any longer and started laughing.

God that was fun.

***

Bailey's birthday came and went. A week later, she came home from school to find her mother on the couch and Annie sitting on the floor beside her. She was using a bottle of pills as a rattle, giggling, bouncing up and down in her onesie on the remains of a shattered wine glass.

Her mother's arm hung limp over the edge of the couch. Bailey felt warmth spread through her body, and a smile she couldn't stop spread across her face. *Is it over? Is she dead? Is this what joy feels like?*

She laid her hand on her mother's chest and could feel a heartbeat. *Damn.* She lifted her arm and dropped it. Nothing.

She reached up and cupped her mother's chin and squeezed as hard as she could. Leaning forward, their noses almost touching, she yelled.

"MOM."

Nothing.

Bailey raised her right hand and slapped her mother as hard as her little body would allow. Her hand stung as if her mother's face was carpeted with millions of tiny needles. Bailey felt the shock wiggle through her hands, up her arm, and to her face. Her lips stretched in a wide grin.

She was glad the first one didn't wake her mother. She raised her hand again, this time backhanding her mother across her cheek and jaw.

Nothing.

It felt good, hitting her mother. Revenge for the times she'd been slapped. It was disappointing her mother wasn't awake to feel it. She took advantage of the fact and pinched her in different places.

Still nothing.

Everyone knew she was home; she'd seen Mrs. Klein on her way to the door. She wished she could leave her mother there, maybe she'd get sick from the pills and the wine and throw up and choke on it.

But no, she needed to call her dad. He didn't pick up, so she called over and over until he got the hint and finally answered. She heard papers shuffling in the background, and he sounded frazzled when he answered.

"It's me, Dad," she said.

Everything in the background stopped. "Hey, honey, what's wrong? Why are you calling here?"

"It's Mom. She's passed out, and I can't wake her up."

She heard the gasp of breath her father

took and could hear panic in his voice when he asked: "Is she breathing, Bay?"

"Yes, she is. And her heart's beating."

"I'll be home in twenty minutes." Panic morphed into irritation. "If anything happens, call 911." The line clicked.

Bailey spent the entire twenty minutes waiting on her mother to stop breathing. Annie continued to shake the pill bottle now and then, and the sound combined with her watching her mother's rising and falling chest sent Bailey into a trance.

I could hold one of the couch pillows over her face. That might work.

There was a small, square pillow on the end of the couch. Bailey lifted it and ran the palm of her hand over the teal, raised design. *That might leave gaps she can breathe through.*

She flipped it over to the smooth side and held it inches over her mother's head. Annie continued shaking the pill bottle, paying no attention to what her big sissy was doing. Bailey lowered the pillow, inch by inch, until it touched her mother's nose.

Her mother groaned, but didn't open her eyes. Bailey threw the pillow into the kitchen. She didn't consider her mother might wake up. If she did, Bailey might not be strong enough to finish the job if she were conscious and fighting back. She'd rat her out to her dad as soon as he walked in the door.

She looked over at Annie. *I could pop the cap off that bottle and tell Annie they're pieces of candy.* She would watch as her little sister chewed the capsules, letting the medication slide down her throat and absorb into her cheeks and tongue.

She could almost hear Annie start to cry at the bitter taste, hear her retching. It was easy to imagine her sister lying there, overdosing on whatever it was her mom was prescribed that week.

But what about her father? She didn't mention Annie on the phone, and he would be expecting her to take care of her until he got home. If he came in and Annie was dying or dead, and her mother was unconscious, with Bailey standing over them ... well, he might have questions.

Before she could discuss it any further with herself, she heard the front door open behind her. Her father appeared beside her and knelt down over her mother.

"Janet." He shook her by the shoulders. "God damn it, Janet. Wake up."

She didn't move.

"Go get me a glass of water, Bay. And what the hell is that noise?" He looked around the living room. Bailey pretended she was only just now hearing it too, and zeroed in on Annie.

"Dad, Annie has Mom's pills!" She pretended to be surprised and concerned, jerking the bottle from Annie's hands, making her cry.

"Her pills? Annie had her pills? Are you fucking kidding me? Janet!"

I am not fucking kidding you, Dad.

"Go get that water, Bailey." Her father reached up and shoved her toward the kitchen, squeezing her shoulder hard. His voice was angrier than she'd heard in a long time, and he was *never* physical with her. She deserved it for not listening the first time. She was back with the glass of water in a few seconds.

Her father raised the glass a few inches above her mother's face and dumped it. Her mother groaned and slapped at her face, inhaled some of the water and began to cough. She opened her eyes and froze when she saw Bailey and her father looking down at her.

"What the hell?"

Bailey shook her head. "I found you like this when I got home. So, I called Dad."

"Bailey, take Annie upstairs and stay there until I tell you to come down." His voice was cold. He never sounded like that before—not even during her parents' *worst* fights. This was not going to be good.

She scooped up her sister and hauled her upstairs. The front of the crib slid downward when she pushed the button, and she shoved Annie down on the mattress. Bailey raised the crib front and locked it into place as fast as she could. She didn't want to miss the show.

Within sixty seconds, she was on her perch.

"I'm sorry, Len, I fell asleep."

"You fell asleep. Yeah, I guess mixing wine and pills can be pretty exhausting."

"I just had one glass."

"One glass that was shattered to pieces while my baby girl sat amongst the shards and used your pills as a fucking rattle, Janet. Do you understand what could have happened?"

Her mother said nothing.

"You're lucky Bailey came home when she did."

"Oh yes, the prodigal daughter returned, saving the family from certain peril." Bailey didn't know that word—*prodigal*—but made a mental note to look it up later. She did, however, recognize the sarcasm and venom dripping from her mother's words, so it couldn't be good.

"Shut your mouth. She's not the one drinking and drugging while Annie wanders the house alone."

"God, Lenny, I made a mistake. I should have waited to take my dose. Now I know for next time. Can we just let this go?"

"Let it go? Do you have any idea what you could have done here? Annie could have hurt herself. She could have walked out the front door, swallowed your pills, cut herself on the glass. This time you've gone too far. Someone could have been seriously hurt or killed, Janet."

"Okay, sure. But nobody was. Can we just chalk it up to being a tired mother who had a lapse in judgment? It won't happen again. I promise. I'm sorry."

"No, I don't think so. I can't do this anymore."

"What do you mean? You can't do what anymore?"

"I can't keep dealing with you like this. The drinking, the pills, it's got to stop."

"I can't stop taking my medication, Lenny, you know that. And one glass of wine—"

"*One* glass?" Her father was yelling now. "*One* glass?"

There was a pause that felt like hours.

"Yes, I had one glass. I have one glass every day. It helps with my nerves."

Bailey heard her father's feet pound across the kitchen, and her mother cried out in pain. The back-door hinges echoed her scream.

Bailey peeked around the edge of her perch and saw her father carrying a garbage bag in one hand, dragging her mother by her upper arm in the other. He dumped the bag onto the kitchen floor, and dozens of bottles came rolling out. Large wine bottles, small travel sized bottles, blue ones, red ones, a couple of purple ones. The smell snaked its way to the stairs and burned Bailey's nose.

Busted.

"Lenny—"

"No, Janet. No. You've been hiding bottles for months. You think I didn't know? That I didn't notice the smell of liquor on you at the end of the day? Or notice the debit transactions down at the liquor store?"

"I—"

"You nothing. You didn't know I was watching the money. And every night I checked the bags outside to see how much you'd pulled in that day. And you know, some of today is on me. I should have stopped you a long time ago. You're a drunk—but I thought you had a handle on it. I can see now you don't."

"Lenny, I can stop— "

"You can stop?" He was laughing. "You *can* stop. But you won't, and we both know it. You can't handle being a wife, and you sure can't handle being a mother. I want out of this marriage, Janet. This is over."

Bailey threw a little party inside. *Finally!* He'd take her, and maybe she could get him to leave Annie with her mother. The two of them could go somewhere else and be free of this woman and that stupid baby.

"I can't trust you with the kids, Janet.

Nothing happened this time, but what about next time? What if Bailey doesn't walk in at the right time, or what if Annie gets the lid off one of your bottles?"

"I'll flush them all down the toilet." Bailey watched as she grabbed the bottle and went into the kitchen. Two of their cabinets were designated for medications, and she took all the bottles with her name out. She headed for the downstairs bathroom, and he followed. They were out of her line of sight now.

"Janet, this isn't going to solve anything."

Bailey heard the plopping sounds and small splashes as her mother dumped her bottles into the toilet. She flushed.

"There, Lenny. They're all gone. The liquor and wine are going down the sink, right now." He followed her into the kitchen, where she started pouring bottles of alcohol down the sink.

"And there's none hidden in the bedroom? Or anywhere else?" her father asked.

The pause is what did her in. She waited too long to answer.

"I'm leaving," her father said.

Yes! I'm out of here! Maybe he'll leave Annie with her. She's her favorite anyway, and I'm Dad's. We'll just split up, and everybody will be happy.

"And where are you going to go?" Her mother no longer sounded desperate. Her voice was cold, and the tears and thick words were gone.

"I'll take the kids to a hotel for tonight."

Kids. Meaning more than one. Bailey rolled her eyes.

"Tonight?"

"Yeah, tonight. I'll see about finding a place they can go with me as soon as I can."

"You can take Bailey, but you're not taking Annie."

"Like hell I'm not. She can't stay with you. No court will agree to let her stay with an alcoholic, pill-popping mother that's unemployed. I make the money. I'm sober. Those kids are mine. You can visit."

For the first time in Bailey's life, she watched around the corner as her mother hit her father. Her fist was closed, and she landed with a *thud* on his jaw.

Bailey felt like she *flew* down the stairs—like she'd grown wings or had a cape around her neck. She was on her mother in a matter of seconds.

Her world went into slow-motion once again. She could hear nothing. She saw her father freeze, eyes wide and mouth open. She sprung off the ground towards her mother. The woman couldn't get her arms open fast enough to catch her, so she fell over backwards. Bailey straddled her.

"You bitch! I hate you!" She clawed at her mother's face like a cat shredding tissue paper. When her mother's arms rose to protect her face, Bailey leaned down and bit. She closed her tiny fists and swung as hard as she could.

"Never touch my dad again! Never! I'll kill you!"

She felt her father's arms wrap around her as he lifted her off her mother. She snapped out of slow-motion, and sound returned to her ears. When she could no longer reach her, Bailey began spitting in her mother's direction.

She felt like a wild animal. Like the lions she'd seen on the nature programs. The ones that grabbed the zebras by the legs. They pulled them down and tore their throats out with their teeth. She let out a guttural growl from somewhere deep inside her. She felt it shake her whole body.

"Bailey! Bailey, calm down!" Her father had her tight in a bear hug from behind. Her mother lay on the floor, shrieking.

"Honey! Relax! I'm okay. Bay, I'm all right. It's okay." He spoke quietly near her ear, and she could feel his warm breath brush her neck. He rocked her until she regained control of herself and went limp in his arms.

"I want her *out* of here! Right *fucking* now! I'm calling the police!" Her mother rose and reached for her cell phone.

Her father let go of her and moved her aside, getting to the phone before her mother could. "I don't think so, Janet. You're not doing any such thing."

"Give me my fucking phone."

"Okay, I'll give you the phone. You go ahead and call the police. I'll be sure to recount the events and let them know our ten-year-old watched you punch her father."

"Oh, really? Poor you got beat up by your wife. But you don't have a mark on you. Look at my face! Look what your little animal child did to me!" She held her arm up, showing the bite mark. "How are you going to explain this? Fuck you, Lenny."

"You've got alcohol on your breath and pills in your system. *My* daughter, as you like to say, defended me. Think the cops are going to send her to jail for reacting to an abusive mother? I'm willing to bet no. But you call them, Jan. Go ahead." He held out the phone.

She snatched it from his hand. "I want that child the *fuck* out of my house. Right *fucking* now."

"We're leaving for the night. Bailey, go put a few clothes in a bag, and a book or something to keep you busy. We're heading to a hotel for the night."

She started to run for the steps and stopped. "Um, Dad?"

"Yes, honey?" He was behind her, heading for Annie's room.

"What about Barkley?"

He thought for a minute. "Get his leash and his bowls. He's coming too. If we can't find a pet friendly place, we'll sneak him in. He goes where you go, kid."

And so do you, Dad. We are finally getting out of here.

Things were looking up for little Bailey. It could only get better from here.

***

They found a hotel the next town over that didn't mind having Barkley as a guest. Her dad stopped and bought them burgers and fries for dinner, even for Barkley. They were sitting at the little desk in the room beside each other when her father said he needed to talk to her.

She figured this was the time they'd start making their plans to run away and never see her mom. Maybe he'd let Annie go back home. She was pretty persuasive and chose to believe she could talk him into it. For now, Annie sat in a playpen while she and her father ate their burgers at the desk.

"So, that was pretty serious stuff back at home, huh?"

Bailey nodded and dunked her french fry into a pool of ketchup.

"We have to talk about it, you know."

She rolled her eyes.

"Hey, no." He turned their chairs so they faced each other. "No rolling your eyes. We have to talk about what happened."

"Okay."

"You must have been scared when you got home and found Mom like that."

"Not really." She crossed her arms over her chest.

"Well, you did good calling me right away. I'm sorry you had to see her like that."

Wasn't the first time.

He took a bite of his burger, looking her over. She knew what was coming next.

"You got pretty upset when she hit me."

"Yeah." Bailey narrowed her eyes and bit her lip. Thinking about it made her angry all over again. She'd never hurt her father or Barkley, so she didn't know where to direct the anger. She hoped he would let it go, but that didn't seem to be the case.

"Do you think you overreacted?"

"No. You're not supposed to hit. She shouldn't have hit you. When you hit her, she deserves it, and you didn't."

His jaw fell open. "When I hit her? When did you see me hit her?"

"I've seen you do it a couple times. I watch

you guys from the stairs. Like I said, you hit her when she deserves it. Like she only hits me when I deserve it." *Let's see how this goes over.*

"Hits you? When did she hit you?" His brow wormed its way into a *v* shape over his nose, and she watched him chew the inside of his lip. He was a lot like her; he had to fight to keep the anger in.

"She hit me a few times. Like when I fed Annie the bottle. And then again when she gave me the party invitations. But I was smart-mouthing, so I deserved it, just like she did every time you hit her."

"Where did she hit you?"

"Across the mouth."

He hung his head and spoke to the floor. "She shouldn't be hitting you. None of us should be hitting each other."

"It's okay, Dad. It's fine. Sometimes we deserve it. I've seen it with my own eyes, so I know she provoked you." She watched him suck in a deep breath, his chest and shoulders rising. He dropped his gaze to the floor and shook his head.

"Provoked? You heard that word from me, didn't you?" Bailey nodded. "You shouldn't be seeing or hearing this stuff, kid. It's not okay. You're supposed to be in your room, not sitting on the stairs eavesdropping and watching us."

Bailey shrugged. It was fun to watch her mother suffer.

"You're learning really shitty things, watching us." He was talking more to himself than to her, so she let him continue. "Parents don't always get along. I know you kids think we're perfect, but we're humans too, and we mess up. I should never hit your mother, and I'm sorry you've seen that. Things just get out of hand sometimes. It's not going to happen anymore; I promise you that."

Bailey couldn't help but feel joy swell inside her chest. They were done. Never going back. Won't see ya later, alligator.

"You can't react the way you did either, Bay. I've never seen you so angry. We have to put a stop to this before it gets further out of hand. You could have hurt your mother pretty bad, you know."

Duh. That's what I was going for. Sometimes you're not so bright, Dad.

This was getting tiresome. It was time to talk about where they were going next and what her new room would look like. Where would she go to school? Would Barkley have a yard?

Her father rolled up their burger wrappers and stuffed them in the bag. "When we go home tomorrow, we're going to sit down as a family and figure this out. I promise. No more of this for any of us."

"What? Go home tomorrow? We're going back?" She couldn't have heard him right.

"Well, yeah. We have to go back and set things right, Bailey. We can't just run away."

"Why not?" Of course they could. It would be easy. They were already packed anyway, and whatever they didn't have they could buy. There was no reason to go back to the house.

He looked as if she'd grown an extra head. "What do you mean, 'why not?'"

"I don't want to go back there."

"Honey, we're going home. We can't live our lives in a hotel room. You love your mom and your sister, don't you?"

Bailey shook her head and locked eyes with him. She leaned forward in her chair so he could see her face in the light. She wanted to make sure he heard these words.

"No. I do not love them."

"Oh, that's normal for a kid." He tried to laugh it off, but Bailey sensed his unease. "I know your sister can get on your nerves; she's still a baby. She'll grow out of that. And it's not so far-fetched for a daughter to not get along with her mom. This is a phase you'll get past. Life will get easier once we figure this out."

"I'm not going back."

Her father stood and turned off the lights. He handed over her pajamas and headed for the bathroom.

"Yeah, you are. And so am I."

He sounded about as happy as she felt.

***

She found herself back at the front door of their house the next morning. Barkley stood beside her, his leash in her hand. Her father went in ahead of her with Annie on his hip, but she couldn't bring herself to cross the threshold yet.

She thought they'd gotten out. She thought it was over. But here they were, going back in there and pretending to be a family again. Bailey would go on hating her mother and her sister, her father would continue to work too many hours, and things would go right back to where they were.

Her father came back and took her

hand and led her into the house. Her mother was sitting in the oversized living room chair, watching her every move. Bailey had a feeling her mother thought it was over too and was just as disappointed as she was.

That was something they had in common.

"Hey, honey, why don't you take Barkley and your bag upstairs to your room. Unpack your stuff and hang out *inside* your room for a little while." The corner of his mouth raised the tiniest amount. She knew she wasn't going to stay inside her room, and so did he.

She also knew he was going to check, so she went into her room, closed the door, and gave it a minute or two before heading to her perch.

"She has to see a doctor," her mother was saying.

A doctor? She felt fine.

"I think we could all benefit from a shrink," her father responded.

So that was the kind of doctor her mother had in mind. She thought Bailey was crazy.

"Maybe, maybe not, but Bailey going is a requirement if she's staying in this house. That child is a danger to me, and she's a danger to Annie. I'm not having an animal living in my house."

"This is our problem, Janet. I don't know what your problem is with Bailey, but this shit has got to stop. You need to be a better mother."

"A better mother? I tried with that kid, I did. Something's wrong with her, and I can't be the one to fix it. She's got issues."

Bailey felt herself stand and walk toward her bedroom, muttering the whole way.

"I've got *issues*. You *tried*." She opened the door. "I'm an *animal*. You want to send me to a *shrink*?"

She pulled several books from her shelves until she found what she was looking for.

"I'll show you *animal*. I'll show him how you *tried*."

Barkley was waiting for her at her perch. She dropped her hand to his head, swirling her fingers in his hair. She could hear her parents still going back and forth downstairs, voices raised. Bailey cleared her throat and spoke.

"Well, the baby came last week. All of my attempts to abort her were for nothing."

The house went silent.

"The smoking, the drinking. The fall I took down the stairs. The little *bitch* was resilient." She walked down three stairs. "Once she was inside me, something broke and I wanted *it* gone."

"Bailey?" Her father's voice. "I think that book is a little too grown up for you. I want you to stop reading that and put it on my desk upstairs."

Her mother said nothing.

Two more stairs.

"The other day, she shattered a vase. I left the pieces on the floor for an hour and waited for her to run through them. Maybe swallow a small piece or two."

One more stair.

"*Lenny* just adores her."

"What the fuck? What is this? Janet what is this?"

"I put Bailey in a closet the other day. I took one of my pills so I could get some sleep without having to watch her." Bailey raised her voice. "I left her in the dark with a sippy cup of juice and a box of crackers. When I woke up, I checked the time—I'd been out thirteen hours! Thirteen hours of glorious sleep! But then I panicked. I was afraid Lenny might have come home and found her."

Three more stairs.

"Baby girl number two. I'm happy about it. I don't know what's different, but I like *this* little girl."

"Lenny, I—"

"I can't believe this."

Bailey continued. "Annie got into Bailey's room this morning and destroyed some of her precious books. Bailey lost her mind. I think she's a little psychopath."

"Psychopath?" Her father.

She read one final line.

"Maybe she'll get hit by a school bus or a truck or something. That'd be *great*."

She walked down the last few steps and carried the leather-bound journal to her mother, who was now standing in the kitchen, her hand over her mouth. Bailey smiled and threw the journal at her. She walked out the back door, Barkley behind her. Her father exploded, her mother was screaming, and now Annie was howling too.

She was pretty sure she'd finally done it. Her father had no choice but to force her mother out. Bailey was hopeful her mother would take Annie, her *precious* little girl she actually *liked*.

Bailey could finally be happy.

***

She listened from outside the back door.

"You have to be the one to leave, Janet. I'm staying here with the girls. Go to your mother's or somewhere, and get your shit together."

"I'm not leaving Annie."

"Yeah, you are. She sure as hell can't go with you. You can't be trusted to take care of yourself anymore, much less a child."

"How long do you expect me to be gone?"

Her father was quiet for what felt like hours. "I don't think you should come back."

"Not come back?" Bailey heard her mother draw in a shaky breath. "Are you throwing me out? What about our marriage?"

"Our marriage? Oh, honey, our marriage was dead a long time ago. We're no good for each other, and we damn sure aren't teaching our kids anything good. Bailey and I had a conversation last night at the hotel. She's seen us hit each other."

"You mean she's seen you hit me." Her mother snickered.

"Yes, she's seen me hit you. And she saw you hit me back. She thinks you deserve it when I do it. And she thinks *she* deserves it when *you* hit her. Yes, she told me you've hit her. That's the environment our marriage has created for our kids."

"She *did* deserve it. That smartass mouth of hers gets old. You should be the one to go!"

"You have to go so the kids can stay in a familiar place. What are you going to do, lug the kids around from couch to couch? Put them in the basement of your parents' house?"

"I only want Annie."

Big surprise.

"Yes, I've heard. Interesting journal entries. It's pretty clear whom you care about in this house. I can't believe you wrote those things down for Bailey to find."

"I'm glad she found it."

Oh really?

"You are really fucked up, Jan. Really fucked up."

"At least now I don't have to pretend anymore. It was exhausting, you know. Pretending to care about her. It was exhausting just being in her presence. She's a horrible child, and she's got serious issues. You know that Lenny."

"*She's* got issues?" Her father laughed. "Did you ever stop and think her issues are because of *you* and how you've treated her?"

"You're right. It's all my fault. Poor little Bailey. Mommy's so bad to her." Now it was her mother who laughed and couldn't stop. She giggled until she had the hiccups.

Crazy bitch.

"Just go, Janet. I don't want to talk anymore. You did this to this family. I know I've got problems—and believe me when I tell you I'm calling and making therapy appointments for all three of us in the morning. But you need to go. Pack your stuff and go. We'll figure out the logistics later."

Her mother said nothing, and Bailey watched through the screened door as she kneeled down and picked her journal up off the kitchen floor. When she rose, the two locked eyes. Daggers of hate flew toward Bailey, and she lifted her hand to the screen, raising her middle finger to her mother. That was one thing she learned from Leo on the playground. She was still glad he was dead, but grateful for her new trick.

She mouthed the words but stayed silent. Fuck. You.

***

Bailey was back inside and on the couch with Barkley when her mother came downstairs. Her heart surged with happiness when she saw she was hauling Annie around on her hip with a diaper bag hanging from her other shoulder.

Yes! Take her! Maybe her father wouldn't notice.

He did.

"I told you you aren't taking her, Janet."

Her mother pretended not to hear and gathered her purse and keys from the foyer table.

"Give her to me, Janet."

"Fuck you, Lenny. She's going with me."

He hung his head and looked like he was studying the carpet. *Please just let her go. Let her take Annie. We don't need her here.*

"This doesn't have to be ugly, Jan. Leave her here, and we'll figure out a schedule later. I don't think you should be alone with her right now."

"Shouldn't be alone with my own daughter? What do you think I'm going to do?"

"I don't know—fall asleep while she uses a bottle of pills as a rattle? Hope the top doesn't pop off and she doesn't swallow them? What are you going to do when she's screaming and you're too jacked up to do anything about it?"

"I would never—"

"Lock your daughter in a closet?"

Her mother's skin turned white. Bailey could see the blue veins drawing lines like rivers on a map in her geography class. She waited for her to speak, but she only leaned in and kissed Annie's head.

"Now, don't make me do this the hard way. I don't want to get other people involved right now. Just leave her here, and you and I will talk."

"I'm taking—"

Bailey's father reached into the diaper bag and pulled out the journal. *She tried to run with it! Probably wanted to destroy the evidence of how horrible she is.*

"Fine," her mother said. "I'll go. But this isn't over. You're not going to keep my daughters from me. You can keep that one," she pointed at Bailey, "but you're not keeping Annie from me."

She sat Annie down on the floor, covering her in kisses and tears. "Mommy will be back, honey. She's just going to spend the night at Nana's. I'll be back in the morning, I promise, baby."

Once Annie was on the floor, her mother lost her mind.

She walked through the living room, pulling family pictures off the walls and smashing them. She threw them across the room. She grabbed one of Bailey and stomped all over it, shattering the glass.

"Oh, Janet, this is really mature. Again with the dramatics."

"Oh, but, honey, this is fine. This is how we react in this house. It's fine when *Bailey* does it!"

She headed for the kitchen and grabbed two plates from the sink. She threw them both onto the floor, and shards flew in all directions.

Grow up! Bailey thought.

"This is a perfectly acceptable way to react to things! React this way and you get a puppy in this house! Do whatever you want! Break things, cuss, cry, scream. It's all allowed, if your name is *BAILEY* and you're DADDY'S LITTLE GIRL!"

Her father finally grabbed her mother by the arm and pulled her to the door.

"Get out."

"And get you some anger management classes while you're at it," Bailey said. Her hand went straight to her mouth to catch the words, but it was too late.

"Bailey Marie! Upstairs! NOW!" He said it so loud Bailey felt the floor vibrate. She headed up the stairs. She stopped on the landing in front of her bedroom door, listening.

"I didn't want to say this in front of the kids," he said. "But I don't want you back here. We're done. There's nothing left of us. It's not good for us, and it's not good for the kids. Don't come back."

There was a long pause, and Bailey hoped maybe her mother had a stroke or a heart attack or something at this news. She was proud of her father and would be even more proud if his words killed her dead on their sidewalk.

"Annie will live with me," she heard her say.

"Like hell she will. I'll see you in court."

Bailey couldn't contain herself and jumped into the air, pumping her fist. She went into her bedroom where Barkley was waiting and collapsed to the floor. They rolled around, Barkley on his back, kicking his legs. Bailey laughed and scratched his belly. Joy filled her heart.

The bitch was gone. Her father was clear on that. *I don't want you back here*. The words rang in her head like carnival music, and they came along with the excitement and anticipation, as if she were about to step onto the Whirly-Gig and spin until her head felt like a balloon.

Yeah, Annie was still here, but Bailey thought she could change that. Whatever it took, she wanted her gone too. Whether she ended up with her mother or in some orphanage somewhere, it didn't matter.

She knew she wouldn't be able to convince her father to let her go, so she'd have to get creative. Annie still couldn't talk. She was two, but she had "developmental delays in speech." Her father had come to her one day and asked her if she'd spend time reading some of her books to Annie, so she could hear the words and learn them.

That never happened. It would work to Bailey's advantage now. She could almost do anything she wanted to Annie, and she'd never tell. She knew she had to be careful, but she could do it.

Like mother, like daughter.

***

Bailey didn't want to visit a therapist. She wasn't the one who was messed up. It was an unfortunate fact she wasn't allowed to decide for herself, so here she sat on an overstuffed brown couch in the middle of a room made to look like a fancy living room while her father sat outside the door speaking with the *therapist.*

The carpet was a plush tan color, thicker and softer than what was in her house. There was a chair across from her the same shade of chocolate fudge as the couch she sat on. She smelled cookies in the air when she walked in, and her stomach grumbled. Before she could ask for one, she saw the wax warmer on the table in the center of the room.

So, no cookies then. *Stupid, lying wax.*

Quiet music played in the background—some sort of piano-violin combination. It kind of made her sleepy. She fought the urge and looked at the walls, rolling her eyes. This lady put sticky quotes all over her walls, and they were all cheesy and dumb.

On the wall to her right: *Believe in yourself!* Groan.

And to her left: *"The road ahead ... lies within."*

What the hell does that even mean?

Once again, she rolled her eyes. She knew what manipulation was. It was a word used a lot in the books she read, so she'd looked it up online. The therapist created this room to *manipulate* people into thinking this was a safe place.

Not today, lady.

She would not be manipulated. To her, the carpet looked like quicksand, and she wished it would suck this lady right up when she came in and suffocate her. Bailey would watch while her hands wiggled as she grabbed at more quicksand. She grinned at the idea of the woman's fingers wiggling like little worms dancing in the sand.

The deep brown leather chair could still have the spirit of the animal it was taken from. It happened in her science fiction books all the time; things got possessed or took on a life of their own. The seat cushion could lift up, and a great big mouth with huge teeth would bite the lady's head off.

Bailey could see the woman running around the room, flapping her arms, bumping into everything like a headless chicken. This time she had to put a hand over her mouth to keep from laughing too loud.

The door handle jiggled, so Bailey flopped back down on the couch.

"We'll be about an hour, Mr. Heron. Knock if you need anything. There's a coffee maker around the corner."

Her father leaned his head into the room. "You gonna be okay, kid? I'll be right outside this door. Do you need anything?"

Bailey shook her head. *Stop stalling, Dad. Let's get this over with.*

"All right, hon, I'll see you in a bit. But really, I'm just right here."

The therapist smiled and eased the door closed, forcing her father to step back. She turned and faced Bailey.

"Hello, Bailey."

"Hi."

"Would you like some water? Some juice? I have some candy too, if you'd like a piece."

Geez, this lady is trying hard.

It was time to put the good girl mask on.

"No, ma'am, no thank you."

"Oh, well look at you. Aren't you polite?" The therapist's eyebrows raised.

"I try, ma'am." *I think I'm gonna puke.*

"Well, I should introduce myself. My name is Ms. Roberts."

"Okay."

Like I give a crap.

"I'd like to spend a little time today getting to know each other. Does that sound good to you?"

"Yes, ma'am." *No.*

"So, let's start with some easy things. What's your favorite color?"

This could be fun.

"I like red."

"Oh yeah? Red's a nice color. Why red? Is your favorite toy red?"

This witch is unbelievable. Favorite toy? Really? I haven't touched a toy in years.

"No. I like red because blood is red." For a moment, Bailey was back on the playground, watching the blood pool around Leo's head and her new sneakers. "Blood is fun to watch. Sometimes it's thick and moves slow, like when you pour syrup over a stack of hot pancakes. It runs down the side in slow, thick, teardrop shapes. The deep red color is ... beautiful." Beautiful wasn't a strong enough word, but it would have to do.

"And the brighter blood, the stuff that's like water, it's cool too. It leaves red streaks and smears and paints whatever it touches, like watercolors. If I scratched you right now, you'd see the bright, thin stuff bloom like a flower. And if I took my thumb and smeared it, it would look like a paintbrush stroke. It's beautiful too. I

81

guess blood is beautiful no matter what."

She thought for a moment before adding: "No matter where it comes from."

Ms. Roberts scribbled something in her notebook.

"Well." Bailey was pretty sure she wasn't going to go down that line of questioning any further.

"Also, I don't play with *toys*."

"Oh, you don't?" Bailey could see the relief take over Ms. Roberts when she changed the subject. "So, what do you do for fun then?"

"I read."

"What kind of books do you like?"

"Scary ones."

"My nephew loves those Goosebumps books!" The therapist smiled at her. "Which one do you like the most?"

Bailey fought the urge to roll her eyes for the millionth time that day. *Is this woman for real?*

"Goosebumps is for babies. I read *real* scary books. Like Stephen King and stuff."

Ms. Roberts leaned back in her chair and raised her pen to her mouth, biting it before lowering it back to the notebook in her lap.

Scribble, scribble.

"Aren't you a little young for Stephen King? Where do you get these books? Your parents allow you to read them? Who buys them for you?"

Jesus, lady. Lay off.

She explained the way she rescued her books from the library trash.

"I don't get an allowance, and the librarian won't let me check out adult books. They throw them out once a month or so, and I pick through them."

"Very resourceful."

Scribble.

"If you're writing that down to tell my dad, he already knows what I read."

"I see. And he doesn't mind?"

"Nope. He knows I can handle them. He treats me like a grown-up. I'm not like the other stupid kids you get in here."

Scribble.

"That's not very nice."

Ugh. Clean up.

"I didn't mean stupid, I'm sorry." *I meant to say dumbass, but I held that back.* "I just mean they're kind of babyish and not as mature as I am. And my dad knows I can handle things."

"I see." More scribbles.

"What's your favorite Stephen King book?"

"It's a short story, not a book. It's called *The Mangler.*"

The therapist's eyes widened and then narrowed, studying her. Her nose wrinkled.

That got her attention.

"What happens in this story?"

"Well, there's this big machine inside a laundromat. And it sucks people up and eats them. There's a lot of blood and guts and stuff." She felt the excitement in her body; she was talking fast and felt like someone plugged her into a wall socket.

"Oh! And it's possessed by a demon! It breaks free and then—"

"I think that's all I need to know," Ms. Roberts said. She looked like she'd smelled something horrible.

That was fun.

"So anyway, let's talk a little about your parents."

Double ugh.

"Your father treats you like a grown-up. That makes you happy?"

"Yes." *Duh.*

"What about your mother?"

The temperature in the room dropped a million degrees, and Bailey felt like someone dumped ice water down her throat.

"What about her?"

"How is your relationship with her?"

Don't play stupid, lady. We both know why I'm here. I'm done with this.

"You already know. Did you read the journal? It's all in there."

Scribble.

"I haven't read it yet, but I did speak to your father about it. I'd like you to tell me about it though, in your own words."

"I don't want to."

Scribble, scribble.

"Bailey, we won't get anywhere if you don't open up."

"We hate each other, okay? That's in my own words. I hate her, she hates me. What more do you want? Sometimes I wish—"

Ding!

"What was that?"

"That's our session timer. You were about to get started into something good there, Bailey. I'm going to give you a little homework. Go home and think about what you were about to say. Finish that sentence for me. We can talk about it next time."

Next time. Triple ugh.

The therapist rose to her feet and laid her notebook down on the table. It was open, and she didn't notice, so Bailey lingered a beat behind her so she could take a glance at what all the scribbles were about.

Probably about how she can 'help' and how I'll 'adjust.' And how weird I was today.

She couldn't have been more wrong.

Celery.

Potatoes.

Tomatoes.

Bread.

Milk.

It was a grocery list.

Nobody *ever* paid attention to Bailey.

***

Over the next two months, Bailey's parents were in and out of court. Her father was now working from home, so she saw him much more often. She'd not seen her mother since the day she left. Sometimes her mom came around to see Annie, but only when her dad was home, and he gave her warning ahead of time so she could lock herself in her room.

As far as she knew, her mother never asked to see her.

Annie was getting harder to deal with. She was up and walking, babbling gibberish sprinkled with a few actual words here and there. Sometimes Bailey wished her mother would pick her up and take off with her for good.

Bailey spent most of her time with Barkley. He couldn't stand to be away from her. If she went for the mail, he was there. When she got off the school bus, he was there, tongue out and tail wagging. When she took a bath, he'd stand with his front paws on the edge of the tub, watching her every move.

Then Annie ruined everything.

Her father was in his study working, and Annie was asleep in her crib. Bailey slipped out the front door with a book. Warm sun was beaming down, and Bailey sat in the shade under the oak in the yard. Barkley laid at her feet, his muzzle between his paws. A breeze blew the leaves over her head; she loved the swishy sounds it made while she read.

She was absorbed in her book-world and only realized what was happening when she saw the blur that was Barkley in her peripheral vision. She looked up and saw Annie holding Barkley's favorite ball. It was bright yellow with purple stars, hollow inside so it bounced. The sun hit the shiny rubber and sent out a twinkle.

"What are you doing out here, brat?"

Annie shook her hand up and down, still holding the ball. Barkley's head bobbled along with it. Bailey didn't play with him in the front yard; it was too close to the street. Annie must have brought the ball from inside.

"Give me his ball."

Annie squeezed it three times. It sent out a cartoon squeal, making Barkley's ears stand up tall. He tilted his head in that adorable way Bailey loved.

"I said give me the ball, Annie." She was walking toward her little sister when Annie threw the ball.

It all happened so fast. The ball flew toward the street, Barkley trailing behind. Annie was giggling and clapping her hands. Bailey dropped her book and took off after him, looking down the street both ways. She saw the car coming as Barkley's paws left the curb.

Bailey and the car's brakes screamed in unison.

He grabbed the ball in his mouth—she'd never forget that tiny *squeak*. At the same instant, the car connected with his left side.

Again, her world went into slow-motion. This time, however, she heard everything in crystal clear quality.

He let out a high-pitched yelp, shattering Bailey's heart. His body flew through the air further down the street. The car swerved to avoid hitting the dog a second time, but continued on down the street.

Images flashed behind her eyes.

The day they met, Barkley yipping at her from across the creek, then bounding across it getting her wet.

Barkley waiting for her to get off the bus.

Reading to him while he rested his head on her lap.

Hugging him tight, talking to him all night long.

All the times his fur soaked up her quiet tears—tears only Barkley knew she cried.

She heard her father run out the front door. "Annie come here!" The next thing she heard was the front door slamming shut again and her father calling her name.

"Bailey!"

"BARKLEY!" Bailey wailed in the street.

The dog was still breathing, but blood was seeping from his mouth; his tongue was out and flat on the hot asphalt. His chest rose and fell in rapid breaths. His hind leg was twisted; his toes pointed the wrong way. The side of his chest had been ripped open by the car's grill. The edges of his skin looked like hamburger meat, and she could see white between the flaps.

Those are his ribs. Those are my dog's ribs, right there in the open.

This time, the sight of blood did not make her happy. It did not mesmerize her. It was not beautiful.

He whined, and his lungs whistled with each breath. Bailey could see tears in the corners of his eyes, which no longer held that playful puppy life in them. They were dark and full of pain.

This was Annie's fault. She would deal with her later.

She laid down on the asphalt beside him, pressed her nose against his, and rested her hand on his cheek. She wanted to hug him, to pull him into her arms and love him back to the Barkley he was ten minutes ago.

Instead, she caressed his lips and muzzle with her thumb.

"Bailey, honey, I'm so sorry." Her father knelt down beside her and put a hand on her shoulder. "We have to get him out of the street, baby. And you too. We can take him to the vet and have him looked at."

It was too late for a vet, Bailey knew. She knew it down in every bone in her body, in her heart, in her stomach. Barkley wasn't coming back from this. *I want to die right here with him. Leave me!*

She knew better than to think he'd leave her lying there. She allowed him to help her up and watched him lift Barkley and carry him to the yard. She was thankful he was there, because he was gentle, and he cared about Barkley as much as she did.

Almost.

Her father laid Barkley down underneath the oak. Her and Barkley's favorite place to read, or talk—sometimes just be together, without a word.

And now Bailey was alone. Again.

The front door opened, and Annie walked out. She stopped and looked at her sister, bared what teeth she had in a huge smile, and waved.

A volcano erupted inside Bailey. Her body went hot, and she was shaking. She bit down on her lip so hard she tasted blood. She looked down at her hands and saw they were stained with Barkley's blood.

All this blood, and none of it from the right place.

"You did this!"

"Bailey, honey, I know you're upset, but it was an accident. She didn't mean to do it. Take it easy on her, she doesn't understand."

"It's always an accident when Annie does something! She knew throwing that fucking ball would send him in the street!"

"You're upset, I know, but you'll mind your language, Bailey."

Annie made her way towards Barkley. Bailey made it to her in time to keep her from touching him. She dug her fingers hard into

Annie's shoulders and spun her around.

"You stay away from him! You stay away from *me!* I never want to see you again! I hate you!"

Once again, her father appeared by her side. "I know this hurts, kid. I'm going to go put Annie up in her crib and gate her door. I'll be right back. You stay here with Barkley."

He lifted Annie and headed toward the house. Bailey went back over to Barkley's body.

"She'll pay for this," she whispered. Barkley's breathing had slowed to almost nothing. Bailey's jeans wicked up his blood, turning the fabric a deep shade of rusty brown. "I wish it was *her* that was lying here."

Barkley's breaths became further and further apart. Bailey knew what was coming. Her mind flashed to Leo lying sprawled on the playground. Nobody was mad when Leo died because it was an *accident.* His parents talked to her at his funeral when her mother forced her to go. They assured her they knew she didn't do anything on purpose.

They seemed like nice people—but they didn't know she never felt any guilt in the first place. She didn't need to be reassured. She wanted to tell them she was glad he was dead, but she kept on the good girl mask and stayed silent.

Someone treated her bad and did things to hurt her. She reacted, and he was dead. It was an *accident*, even if it happened because she pushed him. *She didn't know* he'd fall and hit his head and die. *Accidents* happen. Her life was better because of that *accident*. She now went to school and everyone left her alone. A kid was dead, but her life was better!

And now, her father was already telling her what Annie did was an *accident*. She didn't know throwing the ball could be dangerous. She didn't *understand* danger.

Wait 'til her mother hears about this. That's how Bailey thought about *Janet* now. *Annie's mother.* She would probably throw a party and buy Annie a pony for doing what she did. She hated Barkley.

While Bailey was considering all of this, Barkley took his last breath. She wasn't sure how long they'd laid together under the tree. The sun was falling into the horizon, turning the sky a deep shade of purple, so she knew some time had passed. She turned her head and saw her father sitting in a chair on the front porch, watching her. He had tissue in his hands, and his eyes were swollen.

She kissed Barkley on the nose. "Goodbye, boy. Thank you for finding me that day at the creek. You were my best friend, and I'll never have another one like you. I will never, ever forget you." She slipped his collar off, leaning down close to his ear. She didn't want her father to hear the next words.

"Annie will have an *accident* of her own soon, Barkley. I'll make sure of it."

***

Her father dug the grave at the base of the oak. The two of them laid Barkley down, wrapped in his favorite blanket. She didn't want to include the yellow ball, but he'd loved it so much he'd chased it into the street and was killed. They'd played so many games of fetch. Sometimes, Barkley would take the ball up to her room and pounce on it, making it squeak. She tried to be annoyed, but his sweet face took over, and she'd end up laughing and rolling around with him on the floor.

Now, they stood over the grave, her father propping his hands and chin on the shovel handle. Bailey stood across from him.

"Barkley, you were a good dog, buddy." Her father was speaking. "Bailey loved you very much." He sniffled. "And so did I." Bailey heard a click as he swallowed hard, raising a dirty thumb to his eye and wiping a tear.

"I *still* love you," she said. "I'll never stop."

Her father smiled, but Bailey could see sadness behind it. He tried. "Of course you still do. Do you have anything else you want to say? Before we—"

"No. I said everything I needed to say when I was laying with him." Her body stiffened. "He knows how I feel."

He nodded, and Bailey watched him ease shovelfuls of dirt onto her best friend. The front door to their small house was closed; the curtains were drawn. Behind them, Annie was in her room. She was sleeping; she didn't have a care in the world. In the morning, Barkley wouldn't be there, and Bailey didn't think the idiot would even notice.

Once the hole was filled, she and her father sat beside each other, their backs against the tree. She knew he was worried about her; she'd noticed him watching her throughout the process. *The process.* That's how this night ended. *The process* of putting her best friend in a garbage bag with a smelly blanket and the murder-toy, and then throwing dirt on top of him. Now *the process* of decomposition—a common word in her scary books—would begin.

Her best friend would rot. Even though her father said the garbage bag would protect Barkley, Bailey knew better. The bugs would be in the bag before they got up and walked away. They'd start gnawing on her friend's flesh, burrowing into his eyes and down his throat. His fur would fall off in clumps.

It wouldn't be too long before all that was left underneath the dirt was just bones, the blanket, and the ball.

That fucking ball.

***

"So, what are you thinking, kiddo? You can talk to me, you know."

"I'm sad Barkley's gone. But I'm pissed off too."

He didn't flinch at her words. "Well, honey. It's normal to be mad at God when people or animals die."

Bailey's face scrunched up. "I'm not mad at God." She didn't think she even believed in God anyway. A guy who died and came back and now everyone worships him? Sounded like one of her sci-fi novels. *That's a zombie, not a God.*

"Who are you pissed at, then? Barkley? He didn't know not to run in the street."

"You're right, he didn't. He didn't do anything wrong. This was all Annie. She threw the ball, and he *loved* that ball, so he chased it into the street. If she hadn't thrown it, he wouldn't have done it."

"Annie's a baby, honey. She doesn't know what she's doing. It wasn't on purpose."

There it was. The claims of Barkley's death being an *accident*. Bailey's eyes narrowed, and she gritted her teeth so hard her jaw started to ache.

"I know she's a baby, which makes her stupid. I know she doesn't know things. It's still her fault. She's always doing stupid shit like that and breaking my things, or tearing pages from my books—or killing my best friend."

"I know she seems to be into everything," he said. She thought he wasn't going to say anything else. He looked away, up into the sky, which was now dotted with millions of tiny stars. There was one big one, by itself, and Bailey imagined it as Barkley's star, looking down on this whole mess.

"She's a baby. She has to be watched all the time. And I wasn't watching her. It's been a lot, Bailey, trying to take care of you two kids by myself. Then you add in my work, and I don't know," he buried his head in his hands. His next words were muffled, but she understood them.

"I don't know if I can do this."

She said nothing.

"Your mother and her damned alcohol. And swallowing whatever pill her psychiatrist threw at her that week. And that *journal*! That awful journal left lying around for you to read any time you wanted."

"You didn't know," she said.

"No, I didn't know about the journal. But I knew things weren't right. I found that cracker in the closet that day, and I could smell the cleaner. I knew something happened, but I left it alone. I kept thinking she'd get better, that being a mom was hard, and I was working long hours, which added to the stress. And when you got older, things seemed okay. You two never got along, but that part seemed normal. Moms and daughters just don't sometimes."

"She didn't want me, but she wanted Annie. Maybe I was a bad baby? Did I cry a lot? Did I make her sick a lot when she was pregnant? Maybe she just wasn't ready for me, but she was for Annie. I don't really care, but sometimes I wonder why."

He looked at her as if he'd forgotten she was there.

"You did nothing wrong, Bailey Marie. Nothing. You were a normal baby that cried sometimes, like any other baby. Maybe you're right, maybe she wasn't ready. We were young, and you weren't planned. It doesn't matter why she did, or why she didn't. What's important is *you* know you did *nothing* wrong."

"Well, she's gone now," Bailey said. "I like it better with you anyway." This was what she'd always wanted. Well, except for the whole little sister part.

"You don't miss her?"

Ha! "No. Not even a little bit."

"Well, you know if you ever decide to have her back in your life, all you have to do is tell me. I will find her, wherever she—"

"Find her? What do you mean?"

His eyes widened, and he put a dirty hand over his mouth. His chest rose as he pulled in all the air he possibly could, then he blew it out, long and loud.

95

"I don't know where your mother is, Bailey."

"How? She comes to see Annie all the time when I'm at school, doesn't she?" *What the hell is this?*

"She did, for a few weeks. Then she stopped. I haven't heard anything from her. She hasn't asked to see Annie. Her mother called and asked if she'd come home; she doesn't know where she is either. She could be in some crack house on her pills somewhere, she could be in another country, for all I know. I have no idea where she is."

Wow. So, she didn't even want Annie anymore. That was an interesting development. For one second, she felt a little bit of kinship with her sister, but it faded away as soon as it came.

Still killed my dog.

It made Bailey feel a little better. It made her realize it wasn't something *she* did. She wasn't a bad kid in the beginning. How could she be? She was only a baby. She wasn't even born yet when her mother wanted her gone. It wasn't something wrong with her. Her mother was broken.

And still, Bailey felt nothing but hate.

"I just don't know if I can do this," he repeated, covering his face with his hands.

Bailey slid over in front of him. She reached for his hands and pulled them away. She put her hands—still dirty and stained with blood—against his cheeks and held his face to hers.

"It's okay. We can do this." She would have to take care of Annie first, but after, it would be the two of them. No more bitch, no more brat. Of course, she couldn't explain any of that to her father.

"I love you so much, kid." He smiled at her and pulled her into his chest, planting a kiss on her forehead along the way.

Bailey closed her eyes and thought hard. She thought about all the possible accidents that could happen in and around her house. Sometimes accidents ended in a bloody lip, sliced open by the spine of a book.

Sometimes accidents ended in death.

***

Bailey spent a lot of her free time trying to figure out how to make this work. Everything had to fall into place so people thought it was an *accident* and not something she orchestrated.

Some of her ideas were duds.

Could Annie drown in the bathtub? No. She'd have to be held down, and she'd fight, and there was too much room for error in that case.

She was watching the news with her father one night and saw an interesting story. A little boy had swallowed magnets and ball bearings, tiny little metal balls. When the magnets found the balls in his stomach, they started moving around. The doctor they interviewed said he was worried about *ruptured bowels*. Those could cause an infection and kill a child.

Could Bailey get Annie to swallow magnets and metal? She wouldn't do it on her own, and Bailey couldn't force anything; she'd seen enough crime shows and read enough books to know they'd probably be able to tell if she did. She could try to bake it into some cookies or something—but what if her father had one?

No, definitely not a good idea.

She was in her room, going over her plans, when Annie came in.

"Get out."

Annie was looking at her books.

"Keep your hands off my stuff, brat. Get out."

Annie grabbed a book and ran from the room. Bailey chased her to the top of the stairs.

"Give me my book!"

Annie was laughing. For her, it was a fun little come-and-get-it game.

For Bailey, it was an opportunity.

She reached down and grabbed the book. Annie's grip tightened. She leaned away from Bailey, pulling with all the strength her little body had. Bailey turned so Annie had her back to the staircase.

Bailey let go of the book.

The sudden release sent Annie falling backward down the stairs. She did a somersault—something Bailey could never quite do, and she was kind of jealous of Annie's execution. She landed at the bottom and started screaming.

"Dad!" Bailey yelled.

"What? What is it?" Her father came running down the hallway from his office.

"Annie! She had my book, and when I tried to take it back, she fell down the stairs!" There needed to be a little truth there in order for this to work. She could have left the book part out, but he'd see it at the bottom of the stairs and might ask her about it.

He flew down the stairs, Bailey right behind him.

"Annie, honey, it's okay. It's okay. I'm here, baby." He lifted her up and tried to stand her on her feet. She fell back down on her butt. "Bailey, go get the diaper bag. We need to take her to the hospital. She's fine, I think, but probably really sore."

Bailey didn't move. What went wrong? Why was she *fine*? When this crap happened in movies and books, usually the person who fell went into a coma, or died, or something. Annie was already quieting down, and her dad had given her a fucking sucker to eat.

This did not go as she planned at all.

"Bailey, honey, I need you to go get the diaper bag. She's fine. It was an accident, she's fine, it's not your fault."

She was so sick of that word.

On her way to Annie's room to get the diaper bag, she told herself this was a trial run. It showed her things could go wrong; if this wasn't planned right, Annie would live through whatever she did and it would only be worse for her. Her father would now be showering Annie with love and gifts and attention while Bailey sat back, fuming.

She would not give up.

***

It was fall break for Bailey's school, and she spent her afternoons outside sitting beneath the oak, reading to Barkley. She knew he was dead, but he was still there beneath the tree. There was still a connection between the two of them, and

99

she read his favorite books aloud, often. The air carried a chill, and Bailey loved it. She liked the cold season—fires in fireplaces, gloves on her hands. She loved the smells of fall—pumpkins, cinnamon, baked pies. She would breathe in as deep as she could, pulling all those smells into her nose and mouth, almost tasting them.

That afternoon, while reading to Barkley, her father brought Annie out front.

"Can you watch her for a little bit? She's getting into everything, and I have to get some work done."

Bailey rolled her eyes.

"I can see that, you know," he said, smiling. "Just for a little bit, Bay. Half hour tops. Can you do that for me? Pretty please?"

He tilted his head and batted his eyelashes while showing off the creepiest grin Bailey had ever seen. She couldn't help but laugh.

"Yeah, okay. Half an hour!"

"Thank you, deah," he said in a mock southern belle accent. "I shall return soon." He hopped up the steps and back into the house, closing the screened door behind him but leaving the front door open.

Her father was in a good mood these days. After their conversation the night Barkley died, Bailey did what she could around the house to help him out. She did dishes and laundry and helped get dinner going when it wasn't too complicated. She didn't mind because she could see how much better he felt.

"Okay, brat. Get one of your toys and play over there and let me read to Barkley."

She watched Annie pick through the outside box, looking for her favorite. Finally, she found it at the bottom. It was a yellow rubber duck with a neon orange bill and blue polka dots. She threw it into the air and chased it.

Only a stupid kid like her would find something so dumb entertaining.

Bailey went back to reading to Barkley. Minutes later, a car horn blared, and she looked up from her book. Annie had thrown her duck to the curb and chased it almost into the street.

Her father yelled down from a window. "Everything okay?"

"Yep, fine. Just a car."

"She's so stupid," Bailey said to the grave. "That kid is going to end up getting herself run over just like—"

Like Barkley.

Puzzle pieces started fitting together inside her mind. If she could make it happen, it would be the perfect justice for her best friend. If she got lucky, Annie wouldn't die right away, and maybe she'd suffer a bit, like Barkley did.

She waited and watched the road. Finally, down the street, a blue pickup truck pulled up to the stop sign. The speed limit in their neighborhood was forty-five. The neighbors tried every year to get it lowered because of the children, but it hadn't happened yet. She watched the blue pickup take off from the stop sign, following it with her eyes as it passed the house.

It looked like the stop sign was far enough away. Once a car took off from it, they would be going the full speed limit by the time they got to the house, if not more.

Perfect.

"Hey, Annie? Want to play?"

Annie stopped dead in her tracks and looked at Bailey. Her face was twisted with hesitation and confusion. That was how rarely Bailey addressed her sister. Annie was young, and stupid, but she still knew better than to trust Bailey, it seemed.

"Come on. I'll throw your ducky. Doesn't that sound fun?"

Annie hesitated a little longer, then finally thrust her hand with the duck in it at Bailey, baring all her teeth in a smile. "Bailey, throw."

Bailey nodded. "Yes, Bailey throw ducky. Annie chase."

"Annie, chase!" She pointed at herself.

Bailey threw the duck, and Annie chased after it. Before she threw it each time, she looked down at the stop sign.

Several rounds of fetch later, Bailey saw an orange car pull up to the stop sign. It wasn't as big and heavy as a truck, but it wasn't a small car either. It looked like it could pack a punch.

She held the duck, watching the car and trying to get the timing right. Once she thought it was time, she tossed the duck. It bounced across the street and landed upside down. Annie ran right along after it. For a moment, Bailey thought it wasn't going to work. Annie was going to be across the street before the car got there. She hadn't factored in Annie's excitement-fueled speed.

Then, she tripped.

She hit her knees just before the grill of the car made contact.

Bailey watched it all in slow-motion, the sounds of her world muffled again.

Annie went flying and bounced off the road. Bailey hoped everything inside her little sister burst and turned to jelly. She pictured her bones shattering, her organs smashing.

YES! Bailey screamed on the inside. On the outside, she put on her loving big sister mask and ran to the road screaming.

She fell to her knees over Annie, looking at the mess. Her head was shaved as it slid down the asphalt; a chunk of her scalp and some of her skull was missing. She could see some of Annie's *brain!*

Bailey looked over the hood at the driver, who was still sitting in the driver's seat. He was crying and shaking, his lips moving. He didn't seem to register her looking at him. She looked over her shoulder and didn't see her father, so he must not have gotten the memo yet.

When she was sure nobody was watching, she stuck her finger into the hole in Annie's skull.

It was squishy, like that slime stuff she learned how to make on the internet. Only this stuff was wet. She swirled her finger around in the blood seeping from the hole. It definitely *sounded* like the slime stuff, all squelchy and smacky.

One of Annie's legs was bent backwards, similar to how Barkley's was. Her face was unrecognizable. When she landed on the asphalt, the force pushed her down the street for a couple of feet, face down. Her nose was almost gone, leaving two holes and flaps of skin hanging loose. Annie's mouth hung open, and Bailey could see several teeth were missing, along with the tip of her tongue.

103

One eye was slightly bulging out of its socket. The other was closed.

"Hey, Bailey, I'm almo—"

The yell he produced chilled Bailey to her bones. She didn't think about how he would react. It was okay, though, because she would help him through it, and they'd be okay.

He made it out to the street faster than Bailey thought possible. First, he dropped down to his knees beside Bailey to see if Annie was okay. While he was assessing the damage, the driver stepped out and approached.

He saw Annie and vomited in her hair, droplets misting Annie's face, mixing with the liquefied innards oozing out of her. Her father leapt to his feet and grabbed the driver by the throat.

"What the fuck were you doing?"

"I-I-I'm so sorry. I d-d-don't know w-w-what h-happened. She wasn't there, and th-th-then she was."

"Did you call somebody?"

"Oh God, no, n-n-no I haven't yet."

Her father went to the car and found the driver's phone and dialed 911. The man went over to the curb in front of their house and sat down, sobbing and shaking.

Bailey looked back at Annie. The smell was the worst. She'd shit all over herself. There was another smell—it made her eyes and nose burn. She thought it might be bile; her science teacher spent the last week before break teaching them about the liver and acid and things like that.

If she was right, that meant Annie's liver burst, and maybe she really *did* turn to jelly!

Bailey's father grabbed her and spun her around.

"What happened to her? Why weren't you watching her?"

Show time.

"She was too fast! She threw that duck and chased it, and she was so fast. It landed in the street, and I couldn't get to her quick enough. I tried!" She coughed and blew a snot bubble for effect.

Her father let her go. He dropped to his knees again over Annie, touching her face, wailing. "No, no, no," he said, over and over, cradling her. Bailey saw drool and snot fall from her father's face onto her sister.

Her heart felt heavy, seeing him like that. She knew he felt the same way she did when Annie killed Barkley. The pain filled up your lungs and filled up your chest and suffocated you. And it made you feel so angry. Sometimes, you even tried to tell yourself it didn't really happen. She had a feeling her father was saying that to himself right now; it was just a dream.

But it wasn't. And yeah, it hurt right now, but her father didn't know how good things were about to become.

Sirens in the distance, growing louder as they approached. Soon, flashing red and blue gumballs surrounded her. Her father wept. The driver stood off to the side with police, answering questions.

Bailey eased herself backwards, to the oak tree, to Barkley's grave.

"We did it," she said.

She raised her hands to her mouth, trying to hide her smile.

***

Bailey and her father made it through the funeral. Her mother didn't come. Bailey preferred it that way, and she figured her father did too.

It was a closed casket. *Let's face it, nobody else wants to see a kid whose face is shaved off.* She laughed out loud at her little joke. *Annie can't 'face' anything anymore!*

She'd replayed the day of the *accident* over and over in her mind. The sound of the grill connecting. The sound her body made when it bounced off the asphalt like a sack of potatoes. The crack she heard when her head bounced— that same smashed cantaloupe sound Leo's head made.

Crack, split. Cue juice.

She was going over everything in her head again when a voice broke into her thoughts.

"Bailey."

She was supposed to be alone.

"Bailey Marie."

She left her bedroom and looked down the stairs.

Her mother was there, looking up at her. They made eye contact, and her mother walked away, toward the kitchen. She was a mess. Her hair was tangled and matted. The t-shirt she wore was stained in places, as were her pants. She smelled of alcohol and wet diapers.

And she wasn't wearing shoes. She was wearing purple unicorn slippers.

What the fuck is this? What is she doing here?

Bailey stood at the top of the stairs,

considering her next move. She could run down and out the front door. She could close her bedroom door, but there wasn't a lock on it. Instead, she pulled out the cell phone her father gave her for emergencies. This probably wasn't one, but something felt off to Bailey. Neither of them knew where she'd been all this time, and now she was here after Annie's death?

What game was she playing?

She dialed her father's number. It went straight to voicemail. She tiptoed to her door and eased it closed.

"Hi, Dad. I know you're busy, but I need you to come home when you get this. Mom's here. I don't know what she wants. So please come home as soon as you get this." She tapped the screen to end the call.

Her stomach flip-flopped. Normally, she felt hate every time her mother was near or was talked about. But this time, she felt something different. Something foreign.

Fear.

Her mother was here for a reason. It was possible she'd gone bonkers and showed up because she didn't know what else to do. But Bailey didn't think so.

I may have pushed her a bit too far. Got her thrown out, killed her favorite kid. Maybe her mother finally found her spine and was here to exact revenge. Bailey trembled, hating these feelings—this mixture of fear and *guilt.*

No! I won't sit up here and hide from that woman. She laid her cell phone back down on her desk and headed down the stairs to the kitchen.

Game on, bitch.

***

Her mother was sitting at the kitchen table as if she'd been there every day for the last several months. As if she'd never left them.

"What do you want?" Bailey asked.

"Well, hello to you too."

"Why are you here?"

"What's with all the questions, *Bay*?"

How dare she use the nickname her father gave her. It was like glass piercing her heart, hearing that word come out of her mother's mouth.

"Where have you been?"

"Why did you kill my daughter?"

Bailey froze. So, she knew Annie was dead, no big deal. The whole town knew. It was all over the papers and the news, and the guy who hit her was arrested for texting while driving. Everything went off without a hitch.

"I didn't kill her. That guy in the car did."

"Right." Her mother chewed the inside of her cheek and nodded. "The guy that was texting. His car hit her."

"Yes."

"And what was she doing in the street?"

Waiting to die.

"She was playing. She threw her duck out there and chased after it, and I couldn't stop her in time."

Her mother's eyes swept the room. She stood up and started opening kitchen cabinets. She opened the refrigerator and freezer and left them open. She lowered the door on the oven, popped open the microwave.

What the hell is she looking for?

She went into the living room and took the pillows off the couch. She turned the chair over, lifted the couch and then dropped it. She opened the chest where they kept their shoes near the front door.

She headed up the stairs, Bailey behind her.

She's crazy.

"What are you looking for?" she asked her mother.

She didn't answer. She went into the bathroom and moved the shower curtain. "Nope."

Next, they headed into her dad's room, where her mother opened the closet. She pulled the drawers out of the dresser one by one and dumped the contents onto the floor. "Not here."

Bailey, usually two steps ahead of her mother, was lost. She felt like she should be doing something, stopping her, but all she could do was follow her around, confused.

Her mother headed into Bailey's room. She pulled all of Bailey's books off her shelves, threw her blankets in the corner, emptied her dresser and desk drawers.

Bailey grabbed her mother from behind, trying to pull her backwards, away from her precious books.

Her mother bucked her off. Bailey fell hard to the floor and lay flat on her back.

"I've had enough of you, you little cunt. You will never, *ever*, lay hands on me again." Her eyes were black, her face blank.

Bailey was frozen. A tiny nugget of fear told her to lay still until her mother backed down. This was all new—the fear—and she had nothing but instinct to guide her.

"Aw, wittle Bailey is finally scared! How refreshing! What's wrong, Bailey? You think Mommy's going to hurt you?" She raised her hand and brought it down to Bailey's face, missing by an inch. Bailey felt the wind blow her bangs to the side.

But she did not flinch. She refused to give her mother any more than she already had.

"Get up."

She got up off the floor, and her mother turned her toward the bedroom door. "Downstairs. You first."

Bailey hesitated, the memory of her pushing Annie down the stairs playing out in her head. She didn't think her mother would push her; it felt like there was another agenda at work here. Bailey gripped the railing as tight as she could and took the steps one at a time. When they got to the bottom, Bailey stood by the edge of the couch, closest to the door. Her mother paced back and forth between the living room and kitchen.

"Where is Barkley, Bailey?"

Is that what she was looking for? Inside dresser drawers and closets? She's gone crazy!

"He's not here."

"Yes, I see that, *Bay*. But where is he?"

"He's outside." Her mother knew what she did. She didn't know how, but she knew. She was toying with Bailey.

"Outside? I didn't see him. Where outside is he?"

Bailey said nothing.

"Oh, dear. I saw a spot underneath the tree

110

out front. Looks like it was dug up not too long ago. Is Barkley down there, *Bay*? Is he under the ground?"

Bailey chewed her lip and fought back tears. It felt like she'd swallowed an apple whole, and now it was stuck in her throat not letting her swallow or breathe.

"Well, if you won't answer my question ..."

Her mother walked through the kitchen and out the back door. Bailey followed her to the shed in the back yard. She spun the wheel on the combination lock, trying twice before she got it right. She opened the door and disappeared inside. A few seconds later, she returned, carrying—

The shovel?

They walked around the side of the house, toward the front yard.

Why did she get the shovel? What is she thinking?

They both stopped at Barkley's grave.

Her mother raised the shovel, and dug.

Oh no, oh no. Ohnoohnoohno.

"Stop! What are you doing? Stop! Please stop!" Bailey grabbed at the shovel, grabbed at her mother, tried with all her might to make this horrible moment go away.

Her mother shoved her down to the ground.

Bailey was frozen in shock. Like it had many times before, her world went quiet and went into slow-motion. It took years for her mother to lower the shovel to the grave and decades for her to bring it back up full of dirt. It took a century for her mother to empty the grave enough to where Bailey could see the trash bag.

She tossed the last shovelful of dirt onto Bailey, snapping her back to full speed.

"Aw, that's a shame. This bag is full of little holes. Bugs must have chewed right through that plastic!"

Her mother pulled the bag out of the grave.

"Huh, I don't remember him being so light."

"Please, stop."

Her mother tore the bag open.

It was as Bailey suspected. Clumps of fur, bones, and pieces of the blanket fell out. The smell of rot—moldy bread, rancid meat, dead fish—forced Bailey's stomach into her throat, dislodging that apple and making her retch.

"Here, catch!"

Her mother threw something at her. She wasn't ready, so it bounced off her and landed a couple feet away.

"Go fetch."

A yellow ball.

Purple stars.

Her world went gray. The image of the ball blurred.

Please, Dad. Please come home.

***

She woke up in the living room. Her mother must have dragged her back inside. Her insides were woozy, and her head was swimming. Something squirmed around her neckline. She reached to scratch, and a white lump fell down into her lap.

A maggot.

Maggots-are-gonna-eat-him-dead.

There was no stifled laughter, no fighting a grin. This time, it wasn't so funny.

And when was her father coming home?

Her eyes felt like someone glued them shut. The lids were heavy, but she forced them open. She sat up on the couch and saw her mother in a chair across from her.

She was holding a gun.

"Hey there, sleepyhead."

"Dad will be home soon," she said, her eyes never leaving the gun.

"Oh, no, we don't have to worry about that. Your father is busy."

"No, he'll be home any minute," she said.

"It's going to be hard for him to make it on four flat tires."

Flat tires? What is she talking about?

"Anyway, I've made sure we'll have plenty of mommy-daughter time."

For the first time she could remember, Bailey felt defeated. There was no grand plan; her father wasn't coming. There was no way out. She couldn't outwit a gun. Her mother had all the power this time. Bailey was furious inside. *This is not how this is supposed to be!*

"So, I ask you again. Why did you kill my daughter?"

"I didn't. She was playing. It wasn't my fault."

Her mother pointed the gun at her.

"Okay, okay. She was outside playing with the duck. I threw it, and it bounced into the street. I didn't mean to."

"Oh, so it was an accident?"

That fucking word again.

"Yes. It was an *accident*." Bailey said these words slow and even, enunciating every syllable. Her heart began to pound, and she felt the electricity in her body again. Her battery power had been low, and someone just plugged her into a socket. She smiled at her mother, struggling to contain her newfound energy.

Her mother wasn't expecting this shift in attitude, and the gun wavered.

"Accidents seem to happen around you a lot, Bailey."

"Yes, they do." She continued to smile.

"That boy that died, was that an accident?"

"I only did what you told me to do, Mommy." She made sure that last word dripped with sugar and syrup, so sweet her teeth ached.

Her mother laid the gun flat in her lap. Bailey was getting to her. It was a dangerous game, she knew. She was trying to buy time until her father got home.

In the beginning, fear took Bailey over. But not anymore. She was in survival mode now. She never gave up on anything before, and she wasn't going to now.

"It's funny to me," her mother said. "When Mrs. Klein called and told me what happened, at first, I didn't connect the dots. But later, I realized, what happened to Annie is exactly what happened to your dog."

Bailey looked her mother in the eyes. She wanted to make sure she heard her words.

"Yeah, I guess it is. They both had *accidents.*"

Her mother jumped from her chair and grabbed Bailey by the chin like she'd done many times before. She squeezed Bailey's cheeks hard, pulling her face forward until their noses touched.

"You murdered my baby." It wasn't a question. There was no shock in her voice. It was a cold, matter-of-fact statement.

Bailey breathed in the smell of sour grapes on her mother's breath. She tried to pull her lips into a frown and widened her eyes, trying to look every bit the part of a sad, remorseful child.

"Of course not, Mommy. She had an *accident*. I didn't *know* she'd run out into the street. I'm just a kid. Besides, if you cared so much, why weren't you at the funeral? Were you too drunk? Or were you passed out from your pills?" She felt another smile coming on and tried to stop it before it spread.

She couldn't.

Her mother raised the gun, pointing it at Bailey again.

Bailey started laughing. She couldn't help herself. This was all so funny. Her mother, standing there with a *gun* in their living room after digging up a *dead dog*. She laughed harder. Her father was stuck somewhere with four flat tires, probably saying 'damn the luck!' like he always did when something happened.

Now she had the hiccups, she was laughing so hard.

Her dog was dead, her sister was dead, and her mother might kill her dead too.

Maggots-are-gonna-eat-me dead! Now, it was funny again.

But no, she didn't want to be dead. Her father would be alone, dealing with this bitch.

If she killed Bailey, she might kill him too. And there was no way her mother was going to win this war.

No way, José.

"It was an accident."

"Fuck your accident! You murdered my little girl!"

Bailey rolled her eyes.

"Your little girl. Your little girl. Blah blah blah. Where the hell were you, then? You left her here with us. Why didn't you take her? We didn't want her here anyway! If you'd taken her, she wouldn't be dead!"

It was true. If her mother took Annie with her when she left, none of this would have happened. Barkley would still be alive, Annie would be alive but out of their lives, and Bailey wouldn't be staring down the barrel of a gun held by her crazy mother.

"I needed to get away. I needed to get my shit together, and then I was going to come back for her." She wasn't talking to Bailey. Instead, she'd gone to the mirror at the bottom of the stairs and was speaking to her reflection.

Crazy bitch.

"Well, you got away. And now she's dead. You can blame me if you want, but it's your fault for not taking her with you."

"You were an accident, you know. I never wanted you. I was too young. I wanted to abort you. I *tried* to abort you."

"Yes, Mother, I know. I read the journal." This was getting tiresome.

"But no, you kept right on breathing and kicking me. You came screaming out into the world. I hated you. I resented the fact you were here. You were an accident, but your sister was everything I wanted, right when I wanted it."

Bailey was surprised to find she felt vindicated. She'd known all along her mother never wanted her, she'd read it in the journal. She never loved her. But now, sitting in this living room, her mother was speaking the truth, and the charade was over.

The laughter came again.

"Stop laughing. What the fuck is wrong with you?"

Bailey snorted and laughed even harder.

"I said stop laughing!"

Tears ran down Bailey's face.

Her mother pulled the trigger.

Bailey brought her hands to her belly, clutching it, still laughing.

Smoke rose from the barrel of the gun, and the smell of gunpowder burned her throat. Blood poured over her fingers, reminding her of a video she saw about Niagara Falls in school. It spilled out of her mouth and over her lips. It tasted like she was sucking on pennies. This was way worse than when she lost a tooth.

She could no longer feel anything, which was probably good. If it was anything like the television shows she watched, or the scary books she read, she knew she was dying.

It was fine with her. Her father would be lost without her, but he would be okay. Maybe she was wrong, and there was a God, and Bailey could go to heaven and tell God to keep her dad safe. Maybe she could even help.

Her mother stood over her, motionless, her jaw slack.

"Did you have an accident, Mom?" Bailey

managed to ask. Her voice was weak, and her lungs whistled, reminding her of Barkley's last breaths. She struggled to pull air in.

Bailey was beginning to drift when the front door flew open and her father came in.

***

"Janet! What the fuck?"

Her eyelids felt like tiny weights were hanging from them, but Bailey could see him through the slits, standing in the doorway, looking at her mother.

"Oops," her mother said.

"Dad."

He ran to her, taking off his shirt and pressing it against her belly with one hand.

"Janet, give me the gun," he said, using the other to pull out his cell phone.

Her mother took two steps backward. Her eyes were glazed over, still pointed down at Bailey. They traveled down Bailey's face, down her chest, and stopped on her bleeding stomach.

"Oh, dear. There's been an accident," she whispered.

"Hand it over, Janet." He tapped his screen a few times and held the phone to his ear.

Her mother was silent.

"Yes, hello, I need police and an ambulance, please," he said into his cell phone. "12601 Luella Blvd. My wife just shot our daughter."

Bailey tried to stay awake. She wanted to make sure her mother didn't go after her father. She tried to talk, but could only move her lips the smallest amount. Her body was giving up on her.

She gave in to sleep.

**

When she opened her eyes again, she was still lying on the couch. Her father still didn't have the gun, and her mother was now sitting back down in the chair. She guessed she hadn't been asleep that long.

She heard sirens, the same as the day Annie died, growing louder the closer they got.

"Janet, lay the gun down. You don't want to be holding that when the police get here."

Her mother wouldn't move.

It was dark outside, and the house's windows filled with blue, red, and white. There were three bangs on the door.

"Police! Mr. Heron? Police! We're coming in!"

As they walked through the front door, Bailey saw her mother move to raise the gun. She heard the police yell.

"Ma'am, drop your weapon! Drop the gun! Hands in the air!"

She didn't drop it. Instead, she raised the muzzle to her temple. Her mother hiccupped. The sound made Bailey think of all the afternoons her mother spent on the couch with a wine glass in her hand, hiccupping in much the same way. She wanted to laugh.

The police fired off rounds, and Bailey's world went dark again.

**

Bailey is standing at one end of a wooden footbridge that crosses the creek behind her house.

Yip!

She looks across the bridge and sees Barkley.

"Barks!" she yells. Bailey takes two steps onto the bridge. Barkley takes two steps back and growls.

She stops, her heart falling into her stomach, tears stinging her eyes.

"What's wrong, boy? Come here, Barkley! Here, boy!"

Barkley whines and lies down at his end of the bridge.

She tries once again to cross, and Barkley raises up, bares his teeth, and snarls. She steps back off the bridge, and he lies down once again, whimpering.

"I don't understand. Why don't you want me?"

Barkley disappears into the high grass for a moment and comes back carrying a ball.

Yellow with purple stars.

Bailey can't take it anymore and begins to run across the bridge. Barkley runs toward her. A thin mist rises through the center boards, keeping them inches away from each other.

Bailey tries to reach through. Every bone, every cell, every drop of blood inside her wants to feel his fur again. She wants to feel his wet nose on her palm, the soft lick of his tongue.

She wants to feel his love.

Her fingers enter the mist, but do not come out the other side. She stands, staring at her arm disappearing the farther into the mist she reaches.

Barkley also tries. She sees his snout enter the mist, but it does not break the barrier onto her side of the bridge.

"Keep trying! Do not give up!" She hears a

man's voice in the background, faint.

Barkley's ears perk up, and he tilts his head.

Oh, how much she missed that head tilt.

Bailey feels herself being pulled back across the bridge by invisible hands. She fights, reaching for the mist, reaching for Barkley.

Her best friend, her furry soul mate, turns his body sideways, watching her.

"Barkley! No! I want to be with you!"

She fights as hard as her little body will allow. The invisible hands do not stop. She is pulled farther and farther away. The world she is in swirls around her, the colors begin to fade.

Barkley turns his back, ball still between his teeth, and walks off into the grass.

***

The voice speaks again from somewhere in the distance.

"We have a heartbeat."

ASMR

Before we begin, let me be clear on one thing: I am not crazy. I know, that's the first thing a crazy person says. Deflect and deny and protest. Everything I'm about to tell you is rooted in science. I did not make this shit up.

Autonomous sensory meridian response. ASMR. Are you familiar with the term? You may not be, but you're familiar with the concept, I am sure of it. Have you ever been reading a magazine—yes, people still enjoy print media—and as you turned the page, the sound the glossy paper made between your fingers as you rubbed them together triggered something in your brain? Maybe your skin rippled with goosebumps or you felt a flutter in your chest. You felt the urge to repeat the action so you could find the feeling again, much the same way a cocaine addict goes for the next line.

I listen to everything around me, seeking out pleasant, calming sounds. Someone cracking open peanuts at a baseball game. The scratch of a match on a matchbox. Soft clicks of the keyboard at the office.

You women with your makeup bags, I know you know what I'm talking about. The sound the thick plastic makes after you unzip the bag. You fold the top back, and the crunch

123

and crinkle makes you close your eyes. You spend extra time rummaging through the plastic tubes, boxes, and compacts, even when you see what you're looking for. The tiny clicks and clacks make the hair on your arms stand up.

I know some of you are reading this and rolling your eyes. You've heard of ASMR, and it's all bullshit to you. Search ASMR on YouTube, and you'll find videos with millions of views, each one designed to fulfill a special need. Some listen to calm anxieties, some to find elusive sleep, others for their own reasons. They know the power of ASMR. Those who leave their laptops playing a ten-hour video for their dog because it's the only thing stopping it from chewing through a wall when it's alone. The parents who've discovered it keeps their babies quiet through the night. I'm willing to bet if you're one of those who doesn't understand, I've at least piqued your interest by now.

Anxieties plague us all. We used to be a society that didn't discuss it; we suffered in silence in fear of judgment, or worse, being committed. Today, people walk around wearing it like a badge of honor. People actually have t-shirts that read "I HAVE ANXIETY #SUPPORTMENTALHEALTH." It's trendy to compare diagnoses, to compare medications, dosages. If you could add up the money mental health merchandise makes a year, I'd be willing to bet it's a billion-dollar industry. I'd also be willing to bet none of that money goes to any kind of research or charity.

I was tired of changing medications, trying to find the right cocktail, the right dose. I was tired of spending money on doctors and prescriptions I had to flush down the toilet because they no longer worked.

My marriage was suffering. I was coming home wound up from having to deal with people at the office all day, and I was taking it out on her. Not physically, I never thought I was that kind of man. But I did yell, and I drank, and I made her life miserable, I'm sure of it.

I was waking up every morning and putting up with traffic that got worse every year to go to a job I hated. To spend ten hours a day with people I hated. Because I needed to make money to take care of the person I loved. And then I fought the same traffic home every day. She'd be standing in the kitchen, smiling, happy to see me.

For a second, I'd feel like I could decompress. But then, she would start. She had no one during the day to talk to, so I was her sounding board. I'd hear about the bills, which, apparently, I never made enough money to pay. I heard all about the argument she had with her mother that day. How much pain her arthritis was giving her. How she couldn't believe what happened on General Hospital that day.

I tried to handle things on my own. I never went to her about how I felt—men don't do that. So, I sat in my recliner every evening, counting my breaths inside my head. I drank a beer or two. I watched inane television shows. I read books.

Scrolling through news articles one morning, I saw a headline about the new rage for anxiety sufferers. ASMR. Could this be what I was looking for? Maybe this would be the answer, and I could come home and have conversations with my wife, I could work my daily job, and maybe I could stop wanting to blow my brains out all over the bathroom wall.

I used it for quite some time. I watched the videos of people tapping on plastic, of people raking straws across expensive microphones. Sexy, red lips whispering to me, the sound of saliva and parting lips lulling me into peace.

But it got old. It became less and less effective as I built up some type of ... immunity, I guess it was. The sounds were soothing, but I couldn't achieve the tingle anymore. My arms stayed free of gooseflesh. No matter what types I tried, no matter who the producer was, I could not find the relief I had before. Anxieties took over again, mood swings came back full force. I was lost without my soothing sounds.

Then my wife served me homemade spaghetti sauce.

Yes, I know, that seems strange. It will all make sense soon. But I want you to know what fixed me. I want you to know how I got better. Maybe you're in the same ASMR rut I'm in. Maybe it's losing its effectiveness. The same as my medication would after a time, the same as breathing techniques or repeating mantras in the mirror every morning.

I suppose it's sort of like pornography. The more you watch, the more bored you get. You're always looking for the next thing to excite you. You go from boring vanilla sex to something a little kinkier. You lose interest in that, so you push your boundary a little bit more, looking for fresh excitement.

Before you know it, your favorite video is a woman in a panda costume squatting over a man in a squirrel suit and she's pissing in his face.

You hate the fact you've gone so far. You're not proud of it. You needed release, and you pushed and pushed and pushed, chasing it. And when you found it, panda costume or not, you held onto it. That's sort of what I'm dealing with now.

Anyway, off on a tangent there, wasn't I? I told you, my mood swings came back. I walked in the door, and she was standing over the stove, cooking. She greeted me like she always does, I kissed her on the cheek. Same routine, different day. Then she held a spoon out to me with a pool of sauce resting in it. It was something she'd done hundreds of times in all our years of marriage.

This time, she didn't cool it down first. I'm sure it was the excitement of creating her first sauce on her own; it kept her from using her usual techniques to cool it down before offering it to me. I don't think she meant for it to, but it burned the inside of my mouth like hot coals.

I spat the sauce into the air, splattering her hair, face, and neck with dots of tomato. I yelled at her, something I have only done four times I can remember in our sixteen years together. She cried, something she'd done probably three million times in our sixteen years together. Women are emotional creatures, and she was no exception. She once cried at an insurance commercial that showed a tree through a house with a small dog sitting on the porch in the rain. I heard all about that poor dog not understanding his life was upside down for days.

The tears began to fall, and her breath hitched in her throat. The sound—the soft, quick intake of whispered breath—something happened inside me. Whispers are common in ASMR, but this was different. There was pain behind it, and my body was washed in serene tingles. I reached for her, and she leaned in, expecting a hug. As she got closer, I wrapped my hands around her slim throat. She reached up, wanting to claw my hands away, but failing. I'd told the woman hundreds of times to stop biting her nails. If she would have listened, she could have put up a fight that night. She never listened. Such a stubborn woman.

A funny thing happened as I strangled her there in the kitchen. She began to gargle and gag, accompanied by a small, whistling wheeze when she managed to get enough air. I felt my eyes roll back into my head. My neck and shoulders relaxed. I felt the prickle of goosebumps flood my arms and legs. My stomach hatched a kaleidoscope of butterflies, sending signals down my nerves and to my crotch, which also physically reacted.

I once again achieved the relief I was looking for.

I choked her until she fell unconscious, then stopped. She was still breathing, and I was grateful for it. As long as she could wake up, I could repeat the process and ride the high as long as possible. I was sure it couldn't last—how often can a person be choked to unconsciousness, allowed to wake, and be choked to that point again without dying?

Twenty-eight times and counting, as of this writing.

I lifted her from the kitchen floor while she was out and tied her to our bed. When she woke, she tried to speak, but all she could manage was a hoarse, dry cry. I explained myself right then, so she'd understand where everything was headed. She spent the last sixteen years trying to please me, and a part of me expected her to want to do this for me too. She stopped fighting against the restraints six days ago, so maybe she's finally seen how she's helping me.

I'm afraid things will get stale again, so I keep things mixed up. The human body can produce many pleasing sounds I'd never considered before. You won't find anything like it on YouTube.

The small crack of her dainty, feminine fingers when I bend them backwards. The crunch of teeth being knocked out of her beautiful head. The sound a gel-filled eyeball makes when you squeeze it—and the pop it made when I went too far. The way different areas of the body sound when you slap or punch them—fatty breasts sound different than a flat stomach, a round ass sounds different than a hollow cheek.

The problem is, she's wearing down. And my methods are getting dull, as I feared. I need more. She'll have to go, of course, but I can't cull people off the streets—I'm not some serial killing freak, you know?

I saw a movie once about the dark web, that seedy, hidden place in a corner of the internet. One can find anything they desire. Credit card numbers, child pornography (what kind of sick freak looks for that? They should all be obliterated from the Earth, if you ask me. They don't belong here with the rest of us productive members of society). And then there are snuff films.

The mob is famous for them. Contract killers often record these for those who hired them. The only issue with those as a form of ASMR is the quality. They're often filmed on shitty burner phones with no special audio. With ASMR, the most important, crucial component is the audio.

The dark web isn't easy to navigate. And you have to be so careful; it's not as hidden anymore, and there are sting and bait sites and files everywhere you look. But—hold on. I may have stumbled across something here ...

Ah, yes! Thanks for waiting. It seems we've found what we're looking for; we've hit the ASMR jackpot here. Files on top of files. I don't know the legalities of owning these, but it must be less than the issues would be if I were killing random people. I'm not a killer, I don't really know how, and I'd end up in prison without a doubt. But this guy here—ASMRDUR7658—he seems more than willing to take the chance. And it doesn't look like he has to keep his ... props ... quiet, either, from the sound of these titles. That would be an interesting change.

Woman sawed 2 bits – Handsaw not electric so it's quiet. Prop fully awake and ungagged. Lots of screams!

Man slowly scalped – New video! Prop awake but gagged.

Teeth pulled with pliers – CRUNCH trigger – prop unconscious. Gum sounds and teeth crunch only!

Nails under fingernails, tapping with hammer – prop gagged but muffled screams.

And in less than thirty seconds, I have twelve downloads going. But I hear sobs; she's waking. Her body is tired, and she's giving up, day by day, and I know soon she'll be gone. It's a shame. I love her; I do. I wish I could keep her around. It's going to be strange not to hear her voice every—

Say, you don't know where I can find a good quality microphone, do you?

Knock-Knock

When we rose from the dead, we thought people would celebrate. These are people who thought they would never see us again! They said, "What I'd give to have him back," or "I just want one more day!" Well, that day came, and quite frankly, you Breathers are all a bunch of ungrateful fucks!

A couple months ago, I was run over by a van during my run at around four in the morning. I know: too early, which equates to too dark. Who's an early riser? This guy. And yes, I *was* wearing reflectors on my sneakers and a tiny LED light on my hip. Any vigilant, respectful driver would have noticed me. One heading home from the closest titty bar after draining the tap dry would not and did not.

I never heard him coming. I was tethered to my phone like most people are these days. Earbuds in, music loud—I shit you not, the last thing I remember is the chorus to AC/DC "Highway to Hell." He didn't even try to brake; he drove right over the line doing forty. Crash, bang, boom. I grew wings and flew about ten feet. Smacked on the pavement. The actual impact isn't even what killed me. I would have survived, but too many cigarettes and too much bacon had clogged the old pipes up, and my ticker up and quit in shock. Game over—if you quit now, your progress will not be saved.

I'd love to tell you I saw a light and ran from it, clinging to life with blood on my sneakers and a busted phone screen. Or God himself looked upon me and released me back to Earth to fulfill my Christian duties. Or maybe Satan himself cast me from the fires of hell, back to do his bidding. Unfortunately, nothing so extreme, nothing so extraordinary. I was awake, and then I wasn't. Dead-o. Finished. End of discussion. Fini.

I don't know how or why, but me and all the stiffs around me woke up. Does it really matter? I mean, we're dead, and we fucking *rose up*. Those of us who were buried call it *digging out*. Some kicked their way out of freezers. They tore their way through body bags. Something about being dead has made us stronger, like that superhero, the Hulk. Some of us even match the skin tone. That was a joke, feel free to laugh. Dead is funny, and I'm part of the club, so I can say so. The idea of a bunch of green-skinned, rotting superheroes running around smashing everything is quite funny.

I expected the world to embrace us. They did not give a shit. Not one. Flying. Fuck.

The first place I went the night I dug out was home to see my wife, Sherry. I was sure our uprising was on the news and all over social media. I could see the video clips in my head: families reuniting, drowning in tears and laughter. Maybe the animals came back too, and little Johnny and Rover ran toward each other in the backyard, falling down together,

Rover giving sloppy kisses with what was left of his worm-eaten tongue.

And I was right: Sherry was there waiting.

The door was locked, so I did the sensible thing and knocked. I could have barged right in, but I didn't want to scare her. Turns out I did that anyway. To her, it must have sounded like my fists were battering rams trying to knock down the door.

Sherry's face appeared in the window. She didn't have quite the look I was hoping for. Instead of soft eyes filled with glistening tears, a smile on those full lips bearing her two front, gapped teeth, I got a furrowed brow and eyes full of fear. She wasn't smiling either. She was grinding her teeth, acting as if I'd just waged war on my own home, and she was willing to die to defend it.

When she saw me, she screamed—my mind went to the old, classic horror films, the black and white ones from the 1950s. It sounded as if she were trying to force her throat right out of her own head. I went to the window to try to comfort her. I'm sure it was a shock, seeing me after three years, thinking I was gone forever.

When I saw my reflection in the window, I understood why. My skin was sagging, gray. My lips were black, and my nose was an inch lower than it should have been. What was once a full head of hair was now patchy, most of it probably left on my pillow in my casket. There was a hole in my right cheek, jagged edges rimmed with a black, gelatinous fluid. I looked down at my hands and saw much the same. In some places, I didn't even have any skin, and my bones were exposed. Decomposition is a nasty little process.

So okay, she gets a pass for the scream. But didn't we vow to love each other in sickness and in health? So, this was my sickness. It was her job to love me, and if she'd only stop screaming, I could remind her of that.

"Get the fuck out of here!" Her voice was muffled by the glass, but I got the message.

"Honey, please. Sherry, open the door."

"Oh my God, you can fucking *talk?*" Her eyes grew three sizes in her head.

"Of course I can talk. Why are you acting this way? I thought you'd be glad to see me. I need to clean up a bit, but I'm me, and you love me."

"I've seen you freaks on the news! *You* aren't Tommy," she yelled. "You're a *monster!* My husband died three years ago, and you are *not* him!"

I was growing tired of the yelling. I've been dead, for fuck's sake. The least you can do is show a guy a little respect. She never spoke to me that way when I was alive. It was difficult to control the urge to kick the door in and rip out her throat so the shouting would stop.

"I *am* Tommy. I don't understand what's going on. If you'll just let me in, we can talk about this. There's no need to keep shouting."

She disappeared from the window. Finally, we were getting somewhere. I knew if she calmed herself down and just listened to me—

She reappeared, holding the end of a shotgun barrel flush with the glass, pointing directly at my head. Again with the theatrics.

"Sherry, put the gun down."

"No way, asshole. Get the fuck out of here. Go somewhere else."

"Why would I go somewhere else? This is my home."

"Like hell it is! Go on! Get moving!"

What happened next was an accident. I promise you it was. I forgot all about my new-found strength, and something washed over me, anger maybe, and I snapped. I reached up and shoved my hand *through* the glass. Sharp edges tore at the decaying skin around my fingers and hand, shredding it in places. I couldn't feel it, so it didn't slow me down. I wrapped my fingers around the top of the barrel, still pointed at my head, and tried to push it down toward the ground.

"Sherry pl—"

She pulled the trigger.

The recoil caused my hand to slip, and the slug went through my wrist, and continued across the street. My severed right hand was still clutching the barrel of the shotgun, which was still in Sherry's hands. It hung there, threads of skin and tendons dangling in the breeze.

This time, she had no screams left in her. We both stood staring at the barrel of the gun. I reached around with my left hand and plucked at the fingers of the hand one by one, until they were no longer wrapped around it. Then I stuck it in the pocket of my funeral suit, where it would be safe.

"Now, would you please let me come in, so we can talk?" I held up my stump. "Maybe we can sew it back on, but I can't do it alone. I could really use a hand."

Finally, she cracked a smile. The one thing

I had going for me since the day we met was my childish sense of humor. Silly puns, knock-knock jokes, one-liners, I could always make her laugh. It was why she agreed to go out with me all those years ago.

"Fine, but I'm keeping the gun. You don't know what they're saying about you guys. Otherwise, you can leave."

"Fine," I said. It wouldn't be there long. She'd see I was the same old Tommy I always was, and we could work through this. It would take time to find a new normal, to figure out how to navigate this new world, but we could do it as long as we communicated.

My stomach was starting to growl, and I was hoping she'd still be willing to feed me like the old days. A hot meal, cold tea, something sweet for dessert. She was always a good house-wife.

***

Our home was not the same as it was the morning I went on my run. The walls were a different color, the furniture was new. Everything was rearranged into a new configuration. Sherry refused to turn her back on me and walked backwards into the living room. Once she felt the sofa against her legs, she sat down and pointed at the oversized chair across from her with the barrel of her shotgun.

It would have been nice to sit beside my wife, but what choice did I have? I didn't want to lose anymore body parts to that barbaric weapon of hers. Why did she even own one of those things anyway? We were never the kind of couple who kept weapons lying around.

And I can't blame her for staying away, because, let's face it—I fucking *stink*. I'm talking about the backyard possum that keeps your yard snake-free crawled up into your air ducts and died, baking and rotting in a hundred-degree Texas heat. I'd seen her wrinkle her nose when I walked in. But Sherry was polite, so she hid her grimace the best she could.

"So, when did you buy the gun?"

"I bought it for protection when you died. Never thought I'd be using it to defend my home from my long dead husband, but here we are." She chuckled at herself, and her body relaxed, a little. Not enough to lower the gun.

"Protection? Has the neighborhood gone bad? Did something happen?"

"No," she said. "Nothing like that. Just being a woman, living alone, I didn't feel safe. I'd been with you since we were teenagers, and all of a sudden, you were gone. I told you not to take those damn runs so early in the morning." *Runs* came out in two syllables as her breath hitched, and a tear leaked from the corner of her left eye.

The gun wavered, and the barrel pointed to my left. I followed it with my eyes and settled on two stainless steel bowls decorated with bones. They sat on a rubber mat, and next to the mat was a small box filled with balls and ropes.

"You got a dog?"

"Oh, yeah, I did. About a month after you, uh, you died."

"I always wanted a dog." I begged her for a dog from the time we moved in together. She said it was too much work, we weren't home enough, she didn't want to have to clean up after it. I said it would be good protection, but no, she didn't want a guard dog. Dogs were a pain and expensive, and absolutely no way, no how, would we *ever* have a dog.

"I know. And I know I said never, but I needed someone living, breathing, around me. Tank takes care of me. He sleeps with me, cuddles me, we play. He's not you, of course not, but he's a companion. He would have loved you."

At the sound of his name, the dog came into the living room. *Tank*, as she called him—how original—was a German Shepherd, roughly eighty pounds or so. He leapt onto the couch and pushed his weight into her. She lowered the shotgun onto her lap and rested her hand on one of his paws.

The two of us looked each other over, Tank and I, and neither of us seemed happy with the other. Tank kept his lip curled in a sneer, his nose never ceasing to move every which way. I was full of bitterness, and I hoped the little shit could smell it. He didn't belong here. Why would she deny me the privilege only to go back on it after my death? Was that fun for her? A power thing?

My excitement at being here again, at seeing my wife, being in my home, was eroding, bit by bit. Sherry hadn't pined for me, hadn't kept things the way they were, didn't seem to have missed me at all. She painted the walls that God-awful green color I hated, the floors were new laminate, and already buckling in corners where I'm almost sure Tank took a piss—I tried to tell her, laminate is not waterproof!—and she had leather furniture. For years, she told me how leather furniture stayed too cold and got scratched too easy. Our wedding photos were no longer on the walls. My favorite thermos wasn't by the coffee pot—which was now an espresso machine; what the fuck is that about? There was nothing here anymore that was mine.

There was a soft buzz, and Sherry laid the shotgun down on the end table beside the couch. She stood and pulled her cell phone from her pocket, swiping and tapping.

"Hey," she said.

I could hear the voice of a man, but it was all *wah wah wah* and no words.

"Yes, he's here. It's fine, everything's okay. We're just talking." A pause, while he *wah-wah-hed* into her ear. "No, no, don't come over yet." Another pause, her jaw dropping. "Mrs. Tilson's son *ate* her? No, it's nothing like that. He's normal Tommy. We're talking. I don't think he'll stay long."

Stay long? Why wouldn't I stay? I dug out of the grave to come back and be with my wife, why wouldn't I be staying in my own home? And if I wasn't, where the hell was I going to go?

"Okay, babe." She stopped, her eyes connecting with mine, widening. "Yeah, I should go. I'll call you when we're done. Don't worry." She turned her head to the right and whispered, "You too."

I knew that *you too*. She'd said it to me often when she was around her coworkers. It was saying "I love you" without telling everybody you were taking a personal call.

I love you.

141

"Who was that?" I asked her. Forget being coy, forget the games. I was in *my* house, with *my* wife, and she was talking to a man I didn't know.

"Nobody, really. A friend."

"Sherry ... you too? A friend? Really?"

She chewed on her bottom lip, and a drop of blood bloomed like an orchid. I could smell it from where I sat. It was strong and sent me back to when I worked at the slaughterhouse with my dad as a kid. Meat and blood, all day long. You would think I would never eat meat again, seeing that process, but all it did was teach me how to choose a good cut of steak. My stomach growled again, the urge to eat making me tremble.

Mrs. Tilson's son ate her? Like on television.

There it was. We were zombies. You watch these shows, you see the movies, and the people in them live in a world where zombies never existed. They haven't seen them in comics or movies like we do in real life. The writers create these universes so the dead rising and consuming living people is a brand-new concept to whatever band of survivors the show focuses on.

This is the real world, and everyone knew what a zombie was.

Rise from the dead? Check.

Decaying and gross? Smelly? Check.

All-consuming hunger? Check. But no, no of course *not*. I would never. She's my *wife*.

But ... she's also moved on with someone new. So, is she really *mine* anymore?

It doesn't matter, there's history there! No. I mustn't. Shall not, will not.

She just smells so *delicious*. The same kind of delicious as an apple pie baking on a December night after a big hot bowl of chicken and dumplings. The kind you can't wait to cool, you pull it out of the oven and stick a fork in, pulling out the gooey, cinnamon goodness, and you burn your mouth. But you don't care, because it tastes *so good*.

Houston, we have a problem.

***

"So, who is he?"

"His name is Frank. We work together."

"How long did you wait?" I asked.

"Does it matter? You were dead, Tommy. I didn't exactly expect you to come waltzing through the door again."

"How long did you wait?"

"I don't know, it just happened. A month?"

A *month*? Fifteen years of marriage replaced in a *fucking month*?

"Wow, I don't know how you managed to wait so long. It must have been so hard for you." My head was filling with rage, something far beyond anything I'd felt when I was alive. This bitch, this woman I loved since we were teenagers. I would have done anything and everything for her. I tried. I gave her all I had. And she wouldn't even let me have a god damned dog! But I died, and *bam!* New interior, new dog, new man.

"Oh, fuck off, Tommy. What did you want me to do? Sit here alone and miserable the rest of my life? Wait for the day I died and we were reunited in some bullshit afterlife? Is that what you wanted?"

Well, of course it was. But I couldn't say that.

"Of course not," I said instead. "But you moved on awful fast."

"I didn't want to be alone."

"Well, now you don't have to be," I said. I took a chance and stood up in front of my chair. Tank leapt off the couch, planting his feet, his fur standing on end from snout to tail. He let out a little chuff and began to growl.

"What are you talking about?"

"We can be together again. I'm here now. I'm alive, and you don't have to be alone or be with Filler Frank over there. We can be happy again."

Sherry's face filled with disgust. I wish she hadn't done that. Things might have been different if she hadn't frowned and wrinkled her nose. If she hadn't looked like she vomited battery acid into her mouth, if she hadn't looked at me like I was some flattened skunk on the highway—yes, ha, ha, I see the irony, flattened on the highway, move on—things might have ended differently. But, she did.

"Be together? Have you seen yourself? You're a fucking zombie, Tommy. You're dead. Your skin is sloughing off, your teeth are gone, you're missing a *hand*—"

"Thanks to you!"

"You scare me, Tommy. I *shot* you. You're not my husband, you never will be, and I don't feel safe around you anymore. It's all over the news, you guys are coming back and things are okay sometimes, and other times you're eating people. And I'll never know which time it is with you. Will he try to eat me today? No. I'm not living my life like that. I'm not gonna put you down like some of the others, but you can't stay here."

"So, I disgust you."

"I'm so sorry, but yes."

That was all I needed. Now I could do what I'd wanted to do since I walked in the door, and I didn't have to feel guilty about it.

"Then I will leave," I said. "You can have your life. I didn't mean to come back and ruin it for you."

"Oh, Tommy," she said, her eyes softening. "You never ruined my life. I loved you, I still do, but this isn't normal. And you're not safe here either, if you think about it. This world isn't going to accept a bunch of zombies running around. They're already killing them in masses. You need to leave and find somewhere else to be safe."

She *loved* me. This isn't *normal*. The more she talked, the more positive I felt about my decision. The sound of her voice began to grate on my rotten ears, like rubbing a cheese grater against a block of steel. The screeching and shouting and the condescending, judgmental *bullshit* was too much.

"Well, if I have to leave, can we have a proper goodbye? We didn't get that before."

"Uh ..." she bristled, her shoulders rising an inch, her arms coming in tight to her sides. "What do you mean 'proper?' Because we definitely aren't going to—"

"I meant a hug, maybe, and a proper goodbye. I'm not asking you for anything else.

145

I don't expect you to fuck the dead guy. You just spent all your time telling me how I repulse you; I'd be a fool to expect something like that. Just a hug."

"I don't think so, Tom."

"A handshake?" I held out my stump and looked down at it. "Oh, oops!"

That got her laughing a little, and she relaxed again. She held her left hand out toward me, and I returned mine. I pulled her toward me, gently so as not to alarm her. She stepped forward, and I leaned in to rest my head on her shoulder in a sort of awkward, platonic hug.

Then I sank my teeth into her neck and tore out a chunk of her flesh. She tried to scream, but it came out in wet gurgles. Her carotid was ripped wide open, showering me in a cascade of warm, wet crimson. It tasted like a cold drink of river water on a hot summer day at the cabin where we used to spend our anniversaries. It quenched a thirst I didn't even know I had.

Her hands flew up to her neck to try to stop the bleeding. I let her because there was no way she was stopping that faucet. In what felt like hours, but was only mere minutes, her life had rushed out of her, and she lay limp. I pushed her body down onto the leather sofa and dove into her torso, teeth first. As I ripped at the flesh and layer of chewy, flavorful, juicy fat—she gained a little weight since I died; ole Filler Frank must not be too active—Tank attacked.

While I was bent over Sherry, Tank was pulling at my calves. Well, they used to be my calves, now they were nothing more than flesh and bone. My skin was so far gone, it slipped right off. It was like those degloving photos and videos online where someone gets their wedding ring caught in machinery and it rips the skin right off the bone.

I kicked at him, but his jaws were stronger, and he pulled my right leg off from the knee down. Just yanked the fucker right off me and chewed on it like some sort of toy from the pet store. It was dehumanizing.

I pulled myself up onto one leg, then reached down and grabbed the dog, lifting him up over my head. He was snarling and snapping, twisting in all directions, but remember, I'm a one-handed zombie superhero. With everything I had, I chucked the dog through the kitchen, where he flew through the plate-glass window in the dining room and landed halfway into the backyard. He did not get up again. I had always wanted to have a dog that could play dead, and this one deserved an Oscar.

With the Tank problem solved, I turned back to my buffet. Spaghetti entrails, meatball organs, all covered in a sweet marinara. I feasted on her liver, gallbladder, spleen—I was about to take the first bite from her cold, miserable heart when someone came through the front door.

Before I could turn, I heard a retch and then a waterfall hitting the tile near the door. It sounded as if someone were strangling a feral cat and then trying to drown it in a bucket. I turned, disgusted. It's very rude to vomit so close to someone who's trying to eat.

Yep, ole Filler Frank, here to save the day. He was holding a machete.

"Well, hello, sir. I'm Tommy. I'm guessing you're Frank? It's nice to meet you. I haven't heard much about you, sorry to say."

Frank had nothing to say to me and came at me, swinging his machete and grunting like a caveman. We danced around like those celebrities do on that television show, all left feet and no balance. I was waiting for someone to hold up the score card and yell "TWO!" Because let's face it, nobody's bad enough to get a ONE, are they?

I zigged when I should have zagged, and his machete went clean through my neck and lopped off my head. Frank went for Sherry, but I saw the realization she was far beyond saving wash over his face. He leaned over her, sobbing, dripping salty tears all over my plate of food.

Rude.

"Hey, Frank?" I said, from somewhere down on the floor. See, it really *is* just like the movies. If you don't harm the brain, we can go right on talking and biting and doing the things.

Frank turned around. I could smell the fear, the sweat. It didn't bother me so much, I was sated for the moment, but it wouldn't last long.

Maybe I can make friends with ole Frank, and he'll help me out. Maybe I can get him to trust me. I mean, what damage can I do without a body? I can be like the little goldfish we all had as kids. Put me somewhere I can see the TV, feed me every day, and I'll provide the entertainment.

He looked down at my head as if I were some alien creature that had fallen from the sky. He was speechless, and I had only a moment to charm him, same as I did Sherry all those years ago.

"Hey, Frank. Why did Sally fall off the swing set?"

Confusion and disgust swirled on Frank's face.

"Because she had no arms! Badum-tshhh."

The tiniest bit of a raise in the corner of his lips. I had him. Time to take it home.

"Knock-knock."

He grunted.

"Frank, it's rude to ignore the door. I said, knock-knock."

"Who's there?"

"Not Sally!"

He stood, stone-faced, staring down at me. His right arm, with the machete still in hand, raised out to his side. He dropped the machete, and it happened.

He burst into laughter, clutching his gut. Tears, snot, red face, the whole lot. Hysterical. Then his eyes wandered back to what was left of Sherry, and a cloud covered his face. He bent and lifted the machete again. It was my last chance.

"Knock-knock!"

Dear Cricket

Dear Cricket,

I know you are broken and feeling alone. The other kids are mean. The adults are failing you. You have been abused and used and thrown away. You cry, and no one wipes your tears. You speak, and no one listens. You keep your head down, and you struggle, but you keep going.

You want to give up. Killing yourself seems like the best way out.

But I am you, and I know you won't do that. You're too stubborn. You're too strong. I know it doesn't feel like it at thirteen, but you are.

And that man taking advantage of you, he will face judgment one day.

And we will be there.

We will spit in his face as he lays in his coffin.

And we will hold hands, twirling, laughing.

Dancing upon his grave.

Love, Madison

***

Madison Campbell stared into the face of her molester. It was in full high-definition, larger than anything else on her screen. He was fatter now, older, but there was no mistaking him. He stared back at her with the same eyes, filled with anger. She'd seen that look before, but there was also a dash of something else.

Fear?

She never forgot his eyes. She never forgot his mouth—the scratch of his mustache on her unblemished skin; she could hear the tiny clicks his rabbit teeth made against hers as he pressed his mouth against her, sweat beads clinging to each hair for dear life. One glance at this photo, and she was back there, sitting on the picnic bench beside him.

"Flight 9345, direct service to Houston, will start boarding at gate thirty-four in twenty minutes."

Her head jerked up, her mind coming back to the present. She turned her phone toward her husband Clay and showed him the photo. He narrowed his eyes at the screen, taking in the headline and the face. He whispered the words aloud.

"Small town man arrested for child pornography and sexual—oh my God, Maddy, is that him?" His eyes rose to her face, full of shock and then fading to the familiar look of pity he often wore. He meant well, and he loved her, but the shadow of pity made her hate him sometimes. It was the look a farmer gives a downed horse before he pulls the trigger.

Madison brought her ice-cold hand to her mouth, trying to hold back sobs. She stared at the ceiling, not blinking. It was an old trick she used for many years to keep tears from coming. Her body was trembling; her stomach felt sick. When she looked back down at Clay, she nodded. There were no words.

"What do you need?" he asked. He always asked her what she needed when she was having a panic attack. This was much worse, next level, but she knew neither of them were prepared for something like this—for the past to come slamming into her like a baseball bat connecting with a wine glass, shattering her.

"Can I go, please?" she asked. He nodded. She didn't need permission, she knew, but it didn't feel right to run away in an airport without a word. It wasn't uncommon for her to flee to a parking lot or a bathroom or anywhere else she could distance herself from the public. She knew he would watch until she walked through the archway into the women's room, and he wouldn't take his eyes off the door until she came back out, headed toward him.

Madison fought the urge to run; she hated attention and wanted to blend in. Her feet would carry her four or five steps at a normal pace, and then she'd trot several feet. She kept her hand over her mouth. She was afraid of what would come out if she removed it. She wanted to vomit, wanted to scream, wanted to cry out like a wounded animal. But she was still aware she was in an airport; she couldn't have any kind of major reaction to anything. Airports took mental meltdowns very seriously these days.

There was another woman waiting for a stall, so Madison took her place beside her on the wall, hand still affixed to her mouth.

"Oh, honey, you okay? You look sick."

Madison looked down at the bathroom floor and nodded.

"Scared to fly, huh? I get it. I was too. This your first time?"

She shook her head. *Please stop talking to*

me.

A *whoosh* and the sound of a bathroom lock sliding open. *Please, go, get away from me. Hurry.*

"Hey, honey, why don't you go on ahead? I can wait. If you need something, just holler."

Madison said nothing and flung herself into the stall. She finally dropped her hand, hanging her head over the toilet. Vomit, pain, and fear rushed out of her like a waterfall. It splashed onto the surface of the toilet water, spraying back into her face.

"Oh, she's okay," she heard the other woman saying. "Just afraid to fly, poor thing." She must have been talking to the other women who were probably giving her stall disgusted looks.

She's okay she's okay she's okay. The words echoed behind her eyeballs, threatening to push them out of her head. *She's okay.*

Madison flushed and sat down onto the toilet. She tried a trick her therapist taught her to help her stay present in times of panic.

"My feet are on the floor," she whispered. "They are heavy. My toes are wiggling."

Madison looked down to see her phone was still clutched in her hand. She was happy to see the screen was dark.

Her thumbs ran back and forth over the textured phone case.

"My phone is green. It has a mandala pattern with rhinestones. The rhinestones sparkle in the light." She tilted her phone left and right. "It is bumpy, the case is hard plastic, but the corners are soft silicone." She pinched one between her thumb and index finger.

These little tricks usually worked. They helped ground her so she could retrain her brain into knowing she was safe. Whatever panic she was having, whatever catastrophic thought, it was all part of the trauma suffered in her past. Her therapist's favorite phrase was, "Things *happened* in your past, but they are not happening *right now*."

Except this time, it wasn't true.

She closed her eyes and tried to focus. He wasn't touching her with his callused, nicotine-stained fingers, those short, fat, sausage links with enough dirt underneath the nails to grow a garden. He wasn't in the airport, stalking her, watching her. The door to the stall wasn't going to fly open, and he wasn't going to be on the other side with his jeans around his ankles, his beer belly hanging down over his cock—his *weapon*. She was sitting in an airport, ending what was a wonderful anniversary trip with her husband. They were supposed to be flying home and doing all the mundane chores you earned when you spent a week away from home. But it was still happening. She was going to read the article attached to the picture, but before she did, she already knew her life was about to go into a blender. 'Round and 'round the blades would go.

When she opened her eyes again, she was looking down at a pair of tennis shoes she recognized. Her eyes traveled up the denim-covered legs to the hem of a navy blue t-shirt. She knew what she would see next: the screen-printed, smiling, cartoon drawing of a cricket. Madison stopped and closed her eyes again, so tight the muscles on her cheekbones ached.

This was not happening. Her brain was in shock. What she saw couldn't be there and wouldn't be when she opened her eyes again.

She willed them open and was still staring at the cartoon. Madison forced her eyes up over the chin, over the full, pink lips, over the button nose ... and locked onto her own ocean-water-blue eyes.

"Cricket," she whispered. She had neither said nor heard that name in what seemed like a lifetime. It was the nickname her parents used when she was younger. Her father said it was because she was always hopping about and chirping incessantly.

Thirteen-year-old Madison, also known as Cricket, stood with her back to the stall door. Her face was expressionless, her eyes wide and wet.

"Cricket, I don't—"

"Flight 9345, direct service to Houston, will be boarding in five minutes. Passengers in Group A, please line up with your boarding passes." Madison jumped off the toilet, looking up to the speaker on the ceiling.

When she looked down again, Cricket was gone.

She was never really there. She couldn't have been.

Madison took five deep breaths in through the nose and out through the mouth before she slid the lock open on the stall door. She stopped at the sinks, washed her hands, and splashed water on her face, then headed back out the archway, toward Clay.

He was standing there waiting for her. His arms spread open, and she fell into them.

Neither of them said anything. They joined the other passengers and lined up to board. Once their boarding passes were scanned, and they were seated, Madison looked over at her husband.

"I don't think I'm okay."

"I know," he said. "I don't even know what to say, baby. I really don't. But I will do anything and everything you need."

She stared at him while the plane taxied down the runway, unsure what to say. What did she need? She needed to *not* be trapped on this plane, squeezed tightly into her window seat, surrounded by strangers. She would not be able to discuss anything with him, she couldn't let any feelings out, she couldn't cry herself sick on an airplane.

It was back to what it used to be. *Suck it up, pretend it didn't happen, put the mask on, and get shit done.*

The overhead speaker *ping-ponged*. She used to love hearing it, followed by the pilot, who always spoke in soft, calming tones. This time it made her teeth hurt.

"Flight attendants, prepare for takeoff."

The attendants gave their safety speeches and instructed the passengers to turn off their cell phones. There was no WiFi offered on this flight. All she had ringing in her head was the headline. She needed more information. She needed *all* the information. She needed to yell, she needed to hit something. She needed, she needed, she needed.

But for now, all she could do was sit. Four hours. She turned her head toward the window.

She could see nothing but darkness.

***

The plane landed, and they gathered their bags at baggage claim without words. He kept a hand on her at all times; he touched the small of her back, held her elbow, held her hand—all the things he always did to say *I'm here* without speaking.

Madison spent their entire courtship and marriage teaching Clay how to treat her. He knew what certain looks meant; he knew not to argue when she wanted to run. She left him in the middle of grocery stores with full carts; she left him inside fast food restaurants. They turned around in hundreds of parking lots because she couldn't go inside the sit-down restaurant and have dinner with her husband if there were too many cars, or the wrong cars, or people outside. She sent him out for the mail in the rain after work instead of getting it herself. Madison couldn't bear to be out in her own yard, walking her own driveway, on the side of her own street. Who was watching? What would they do? What were they thinking?

A knock would fall on the door—maybe it was the UPS guy delivering her packages from Amazon—the ones she couldn't force herself to go out into public stores and buy. The worst ones were the unannounced people trying to sell her everything from cleaning products to religion. They never took no for an answer and applied so much pressure, she wanted to vomit on their shoes.

Knock, knock, knock. Madison would sit on her couch, frozen in fear. When she unfroze, she would tiptoe to the kitchen. She would pull a knife out of the block near the sink. Her heart would be pounding in her chest so loud she was afraid they would hear it outside the house. The knife gripped in her hand, sweat on her brow, she would wait, facing the door, refusing to be surprised or caught off guard.

Those were the bad days. Sometimes she had good days; her psychiatrist made sure those happened as often as possible with several different prescriptions. She never wanted to be a slave to the pharmaceutical industry, but her only other choice, in her mind, was to die. She couldn't live in her own home afraid of everyone and everything every day; being a recluse wasn't an option. She would rather be dead.

Madison moved through the airport on autopilot while Clay handled the baggage and got them to their car in the garage. The slam of the car door snapped her back to the present.

"I need to read the article." She looked down at her dark phone screen. While everyone else turned theirs back on after landing—all of the pings and dings and musical notes going off around her—she wanted to throw hers across the tarmac rather than power it back up.

"That's up to you, babe," Clay said. "You don't have to do anything you don't want to do. It can wait until morning. You don't have to do it at all."

"I do."

"Okay. Do you need to do it now?"

"I ..." The tears started falling, making ponds on her phone screen and leaving dark

159

spots on her jeans.

"Hey, it's okay. It's okay." He slid his hand over hers, both of them resting on her thigh. "I'm going to drive toward the house. If you need me to pull over, you say the word, and I'll find a spot, and we'll read it together, if you want. Or you can read it to yourself. All you have to do is say the word."

The rest of the way home, Madison went over the possible outcomes of reading the article. Seeing the photo and reading the headline already set her off. There was no rewinding that tape. This wasn't a Choose-Your-Own-Adventure Book; she couldn't flip back to page seventy-two and get a different outcome.

Madison had a feeling reading this would force her to process what happened to her. The adults around her ignored it—*she* tried her best to ignore it, to move on. Yeah, it showed in all her anxieties and fears, but it was personal to her, and nobody else knew why she was the way she was.

But the words on the screen could change everything. There was no choice; she needed the information. And if someone needed her, if there was another little girl, her story might be needed to help end this. She had to read the article.

When she looked up from the dark screen, she was staring at the interior of her garage. She wasn't sure how long they'd been there, but Clay still held her hand.

"I have to read it," she said.

"Okay. Let's do it."

***

160

It turned out she wasn't the only one. She was one of many over a period of decades. It was all in the article. Bobby Lawrence Caine—respected community member, church-goer extraordinaire, mentor to troubled youth—was a child molester and maker of kiddie porn.

He was the smiling church greeter, collector-of-tithes, hugger-of-all. He was the "come forward and I will lay hands on you in prayer" type. The suit-wearing wolf, his sheep's clothing ironed and starched, in the corner watching the little girls in their yellow and pink Easter dresses, snapping photos here and there.

Bobby volunteered as a mentor for troubled youth in the community, wanting to be the "father-figure these kids need." He took them on weekly ice cream runs, trips to the zoo. He babysat the neighbor's kids, and everyone called him "Uncle."

He was on several boards and committees in town. Everyone recognized him, and most loved him. Once in a while, you'd hear a whisper.

It's awful strange he's always with a young girl, isn't it?

No grown man should be babysitting a five- or six-year-old neighbor alone.

Did you see the way he looked at that little girl at the wave pool?

But that didn't matter. Of *course* there was nothing untoward going on. Not in their small town, no sir, not ever. *We don't have those kinds of people here* was the mentality. And definitely not Bobby. No way. He didn't look like some pervert. And he's a pillar in this community!

Madison knew different. She knew the man the whisperers spoke of. She knew the callused hands, the mustached lips, the boozy breath. She knew the flash of an old Polaroid, the mechanical whirring sound it made as the undeveloped photo spit itself out. She knew the nasty words, the threats, the fear he instilled in those weaker than him. Those he could manipulate.

She read the last line of the article over and over again, out loud to Clay.

"If anyone has any information regarding this case, or you know of any victims, please reach out to the Cannel County Police Department."

Madison looked at Clay, and he turned sideways to face her.

"I have to do this. You know I have to," she said.

"I understand. I just want you to be prepared for what comes after."

She'd thought about this many times over the years. If she had come forward all those years ago—or near the end of the statute of limitations as an adult—the tiny community would have had a dark cloud cast over it, and she would be the bringer of the cloud. She would have some support from the whisperers, but that would be all. The others in the town, the many friends and family Bobby had, would try to destroy her.

For years, Madison watched the news, women coming forward after the fact, and saw how they were ripped apart by newscasters and armchair detectives on social media. It was always, "Why'd she wait so long if it really happened?" "There's no proof after all this time." "She just wants attention, or a fat settlement." Those and many more were the reasons women didn't come forward.

They were the reasons *she* didn't come forward all those years ago.

Now was different. Now, with the words in black and white on her phone screen, now, with the details of the things they found inside his home, now knowing there were many more besides her; *now* was the time she was meant to show her face and tell her story.

Madison, along with whomever else came forward, would hammer the nails into his coffin. They would finally end this for all others who would have become victims. He would *never* put his hands on another girl.

One way or another, Madison would make sure of it. She owed it to herself.

She owed it to Cricket.

***

After Clay left for work Monday morning, Madison sat on the couch with the phone in her hand. Her mind raced with all the possible outcomes from making this one phone call.

Could she stay anonymous? Or would everyone in the small town she spent her teenage years in know what happened? Would the details stay hidden in a file somewhere, or would they be plastered all over the news for everyone to gawk at?

The police might not even believe her. She was talking about something that happened decades ago. Would they think she was trying to get attention? Madison watched the news every day and she saw how women in her position were treated. They were eviscerated by social media, political pundits, and the people they thought were their friends and family. Could Madison withstand the scrutiny and trolling that would come along with her story?

Think of the children, Madison thought.

Yes, the children. Years of children he took advantage of. It was too late for her, but it wasn't for the little girl he might run into at the park. Or church. Or anywhere else he chose to harvest from.

It wasn't too late for them.

Whether she could withstand the scrutiny, whatever people around her said, or did or didn't believe, it wasn't too late for them, and she could be a part of stopping it. If it weren't for the children who would be next in line, Madison would have continued to suffer on her own. But because of them, there wasn't a choice.

She dialed the number on the press release.

***

"Cannel Police Department. Can I help you?" The woman who answered sounded sweet, older, almost like a grandmother. For a brief moment, Madison felt a comfort, but it flew away as quickly as it came.

She opened her mouth to speak, then closed it again. She felt her morning smoothie rise up her throat, chunks of banana and strawberry swimming around inside her mouth. *No. You are not going to do this!* Madison

164

swallowed it back down.

"Is someone there? Can I help you?"

"I'm sorry," Madison answered. "My name is Madison, and I'm calling about a story I read. You guys asked if anyone had information to come forward."

"Okay, ma'am. What case is this in reference to?"

She'd have to say his name. It hadn't left her lips in years. Her hands trembled and her phone slipped.

"Oh, um." *Don't clam up now. The children.* "The, uh, Bobby Caine case."

Madison thought she heard a sharp intake of air across the line.

"Oh, yes, ma'am. Of course. We appreciate you calling. I'll need to send you to the detective on the case. Do you mind holding? This is a priority case; it shouldn't take long."

A priority case. Now it's a priority. It wasn't a priority when she tried to tell people about it when she was younger. But *now* it was.

"Sure."

There was a click and a couple of beats of music, then an answer. A man's voice. Strong, but still somehow soft.

"Hello, Detective Hall. I understand you have information on the Caine case?"

All business, no small talk. Right to the point. She guessed that was a good thing, it forced her not to dawdle and stall.

"Yes, sir. I do."

"Okay, ma'am, what's your name?"

"Madison Campbell."

"Okay, Madison, whatcha got for me?" He sounded tired, like this was the hundredth time he'd had this conversation. Police always said they had tip after tip on their cases, but most were dead ends. She imagined he thought the same about her. Maybe it was a mistake calling. Who cared what she had to say this many years later anyway?

Madison raised her left hand and moved it toward the phone, ready to end the call. An unseen force pushed it back down into her lap, as if her hand was a paperclip and her lap was an industrial strength magnet. When she looked, she saw the young hands she recognized at the airport. The ones with the nails bitten to the quick. *Hers.*

"Ma'am?" The detective said. She heard the frustration in his voice.

"I am a victim of Bobby Lawrence Caine." Madison spit it out in one long breath.

She heard the sound of a chair squeaking in the background and saw him sit up straight in her mind. He asked her a couple of questions, feeling out whether this could be an actual lead. The detective must have been pleased with what he heard because he asked her to come down for a formal interview.

"I ..." She trailed off. It wasn't a surprise; of course, they wanted to talk to her. This is why she came forward. At the same time, it still sent an electric shock through her system. Madison knew she'd need to tell the story. They would want all the details, and those details would hopefully help put him away. But now that it was real, and not only in her head, she was frozen. The shame she felt as a child washed over her again. She felt dirty—the kind of dirty that doesn't wash off no matter how many showers you take.

She felt the shackles of guilt slip around her wrists, weighing her down—*what if I had turned him in in the first place?* The other side of her mind tried to tell her she *did*. Someone heard her talking about it and went to her aunt. Nobody did anything to help her. She was lost in a sea of people who were *taking care of her* in all the wrong ways. The adults in her life failed her.

"Madison? You there?"

She still couldn't speak.

"Listen, Mrs. Campbell, I know this is difficult. And I know it's gonna hurt like hell. But so far, you're the only other person we have, besides the original complainant. Anything you have for us would be an immense help in locking this bastard up."

Lock the bastard up. She pictured Bobby behind bars, getting run through by the other inmates, much in the same way she was treated by him. *Yes. Lock him up.*

"Yes, sir. Sorry. When would you like me to come down?"

"Well," the detective said, "how about right now?"

And so it began.

＊＊＊

A few miles down the road, on her way to the police station, a song blared from the speakers. It was about a young girl who was abused, like her. The girl got her own revenge by putting a bullet in the guy's head.

Madison had something to say, and it

would change everything. Not only for her, but hopefully for his other victims, and the ones he would never get to. It would change her marriage, her friendships, and she hoped it would change her outlook.

Madison was tired of the sleepless nights. The nightmares began as soon as the ... events ... started happening. Even once she'd gotten away from him, he still accosted her in her dreams. She spent the nights of her teenage years—her adult years too—trying to work out what she did to make it happen. She didn't dress provocatively. She was outgoing, friendly—maybe she was flirty? He wasn't the first to touch her, and he wasn't the last. Maybe that was all she was good for. All those thoughts, and many more, kept her eyes wide open at night.

Madison was screaming the lyrics, tears running down her cheeks. She could feel her throat get raw with each shriek. Her stomach lurched, but did not produce anything. The car was parked in the police station parking lot; she'd gone the whole drive on autopilot. Her therapist called it "dissociation." Well, she dissociated the *fuck* out of that drive. She hardly remembered putting the car into drive.

She reached into her glove box and pulled out old fast food napkins. They scratched her face like sandpaper, bringing her back to her senses. The napkins absorbed the tears leaking from her eyes and runnels of snot from her nose. She looked at herself in the visor mirror.

I'm an absolute mess.

The makeup she'd put on to hide the previous night's sleeplessness was almost washed off. She swiped pink lip gloss over her too-pale lips and pinched her cheeks for color. Her eyes weren't too bad, thanks to waterproof mascara. It was the little things in life.

Madison Campbell gathered her purse and her phone, then opened her car door. When her feet hit the ground, she told herself:

This is the first step to freedom.
To retribution.

***

The lobby of the police station was empty. She approached the window, and it slid open to reveal the woman who'd answered the phone earlier.

She looked to be in her seventies, and her badge read "Swanson." Madison's mind went to hot, oven-baked pot pies. Her first impression was right, this woman could have been her grandmother. She had a warm face, wore slightly too much makeup, and smelled of old flowers. Again, the comfort she felt was fleeting.

"Yes, ma'am, I'm Madison Campbell. I'm here to see Detective Hall."

"Sure, sweetie," the woman said, somehow smiling and frowning at once. "He'll be just a minute. Take a seat over there, and I'll let you know when he's ready for you."

Madison headed for a corner—she always sat in a corner if she could help it. The two walls made her feel boxed in, safe. Nobody could sneak up behind her, and she wasn't sitting out in the open. She was always on hyper alert status, overly aware of everything and everyone around her. Corners, restaurant booths, and seats near exits were always good choices.

She wished she'd grabbed her jacket from the backseat of her car. The station was like a walk-in freezer. Her fingers and nose were numb. Her teeth made tiny clicking sounds in her ears as they chattered.

Moments later, a door on her left opened, and a short, stocky man in uniform walked through, holding the door to a hallway open. On the other side of the threshold stood a young woman, close to Madison's age, wearing a police department branded t-shirt and jeans. Both had guns on their hips.

"Here she is," Mrs. Swanson sung. "Mrs. Campbell, they're ready for you. If you need anything, you just let me know, sweetheart."

Honey, sweetie, sweetheart. She hated those names. Those were his names.

"Thank you."

"Mrs. Campbell," the man said, extending his arm for a handshake. "I'm Detective Hall. Thank you for coming in today."

Madison put her hand in his and couldn't control the shaking. He laid his left hand over hers and held it steady.

"You're going to be okay," he said.

She pulled her hand back. The only man Madison tolerated touching her, holding her hand, holding her, was Clay. She was not a fan of holding hands or being stroked or hugged—harmless or otherwise.

He gestured toward the door, and the woman got out of the way. Madison walked through, and Detective Hall closed the lobby door behind her.

"This is Hailey Spencer. She's an officer here, training to be a detective. I thought you might be more comf—"

"Hi, Madison," Hailey interrupted. "I'm just here for moral support, if you want me to be. If you don't, I understand. I've been in your shoes and know how difficult this is going to be. I thought if you wanted a female presence in the room, it might be easier."

Madison's eyes flicked to Detective Hall, who was staring at the floor.

There was something about Hailey that made her comfortable—she wore no makeup, had her hair in a ponytail, and seemed sympathetic without oozing pity. It couldn't hurt to have an ally in the room.

"I'd like that," Madison said.

Detective Hall's head snapped up. "That's great. If you're ready, I have an interview room set up down the hall."

The hallway was a long, narrow corridor with doors on each side, every four or five feet. Some were closed. Some held conference tables, dry erase boards, bulletin boards with photos. There might be one or two men in the room, drinking coffee and chuckling.

"This isn't anything like it is on television," Madison said. The quiet between the three of them was unnerving.

"No, no it's not," the detective laughed. "Sometimes things can get exciting, like you see on television, but mostly, it's just us sitting around shuffling paperwork. The excitement is out on the streets."

"I suppose that makes sense," Madison said.

Detective Hall walked a few paces ahead, leaving Hailey behind with Madison.

"Listen, if you need me, or you need to stop, you let me know. I know we don't know each other, but I'm your best friend today. You want a red light, you tell me, and this is over until you're ready again. We have all the time you need."

Madison swallowed a sob-filled ball of tears.

"Thank you," she said.

Ahead, Detective Hall was stopped in front of an open door. He gestured for the two women to follow him inside.

Madison was expecting something out of a television crime drama. She expected to be taken to a large room with a two-way mirror and a large table in the middle. She expected to sit alone in a metal chair, across from the police, underneath a lone light.

Instead, it was worse. She would have preferred the openness of the interrogation room over this—the room was an eight-foot square box, which was about to accommodate three full-grown adults. The walls were made out of acoustic panels, she recognized the material and framework from a symphonic hall she and Clay visited a few times a year. The panel fabric was a drab brown, the carpet matched, and there was one tiny table pushed against the wall on the right. On it was a white legal pad and a pen.

Claustrophobic as fuck.

She looked at Hailey and then around the room.

"I know, tight quarters," Hailey said. "We can arrange somewhere else if we need to."

No, it was too early to start making special demands like she was some sort of delicate flower needing proper humidity and misting and space or she'd shrivel up and die. People did this all the time. There was no reason she couldn't.

"It's fine in here," Madison said. She sat down on her side of the small desk, and Detective Hall took his side. Hailey sat in a chair in the corner, angled to face her.

Cricket appeared again, beside her.

What's she doing here?

She did her best not to react. The detectives would not understand, and she feared it would muck up her credibility if she tried to explain she saw a ghost version of her younger self. It didn't make her seem like a reliable source.

"Are you comfortable, Mrs. Campbell?"

"Call me Madison. And yes, I'm okay."

"Okay, Madison. We need to get a couple of formalities out of the way. A few basic questions to establish who you are and why you're here."

She nodded.

"I'm Detective William Hall. With me is Detective Hailey Spencer. And seated across from me is Madison Campbell."

At first it was strange, listening to him announce the three of them as if someone were watching. Then it dawned on her, the acoustic paneled walls, the lack of a computer or tape recorder—if someone wasn't watching right this second, they'd be able to later, because it was all being recorded. The telltale black bubble was in the corner of the ceiling. It made her slightly uncomfortable, having unseen eyes looking down on her.

Hailey must have noticed her gaze land

on the camera.

"This is being recorded, for our benefit and yours, Madison. Nobody's watching in re-al-time, but it's being saved. It's a non-negotiable part of the process, but I promise you, the footage is protected."

Madison sighed and turned her gaze back to Hall.

"Now, Madison, can you tell me why you're here?"

"The Bobby Caine case. I was a victim of his, years ago."

"Okay, and for the sake of proper identity," he shuffled a few pages on his pad and pulled out five glossy, black and white photos of faces.

Madison's eyes went straight to Cricket, still standing beside Hailey. It was convenient, because Hailey thought she was looking to her for support.

"Hey, I know, he's the last person you want to see. But we have to identify him so there's never any doubt you know who he is and we have him. You going to be okay?"

I don't want to, Madison sent to Cricket.

You have to, Cricket sent back.

So, they could communicate. She wasn't sure if it was a good thing or a bad thing.

It's finally time, Cricket said. *Make the fucker pay. It hurts now, but it will feel so good later.*

"Go ahead." Hall laid the photos out side by side, two on the top row, three on the bottom.

"Can you point out the man you're saying assaulted you as a child?"

She didn't even notice the others, only Bobby Caine and his beady eyes staring back at her, a smirk playing on his lips. It was as if he were taunting her.

Go ahead and try it, sweetheart. She heard him say in her head. *Nobody's gonna believe a God-damned word you got to say this late in the game, babe. Prove it!*

"That's him. Bobby Lawrence Caine." She pointed at him.

Detective Hall gathered the photos up and hid them back in the legal pad.

"Okay, thank you for that, I know that wasn't easy."

You don't know anything, Cricket sent, louder than the last message.

"When did Mr. Caine assault you, Mrs. Campbell?"

"When I was thirteen."

"And how did you two know each other?"

Madison looked back at Cricket. The little girl raised a finger to the wall and pointed. Her nails were bitten to the quick, scabbed skin and swollen cuticles. Madison looked down at her adult hands and found the same.

Look, Cricket said.

She looked up and watched Cricket draw a circle in the wall. When the circle was complete, the view changed, as if looking through a window.

***

Madison snuck out when no one was looking and sat down on a picnic bench beside the church reception hall, alone. The congregation, their friends and family, and random strangers were gathered inside, chowing down on five-dollar barbecue plates cooked by the leaders. The money was slated to be given to the youth group for camp.

Bobby exited the church out the back door and sat down beside her on the bench.

"Hey, kiddo, whatcha up to?"

"Nothing really," she said. The whole point of sneaking out was so she could be alone. She wanted to tell him to go back inside, but children don't tell adults what to do.

"Haven't seen you down here in a while. I'm real sorry about your folks."

She was tired of hearing it. Two years had passed since her parents were killed in the car wreck, and at least once a week, it seemed someone was "sorry for her loss." She lived with an aunt now who didn't pay much attention to her, and she liked it that way. She was on her own. If *she* was fine, Madison felt *they* should be too. The pity and sad faces everyone carried around irritated her. But Bobby approached her that day in a different way. He was warm and friendly in a way that made her relax. She'd heard all her life some people were just good with kids, and he must be one of those people.

"Thanks."

"Well," he said, putting his hand on her bare knee, "if you need anything," his sweet voice faded to a whisper, "Uncle Bobby's here for ya." His finger drew circles on her kneecap.

Something felt off. The way he was breathing, shallow and fast. His eyes traveled up and down her torso. Every now and then, he squeezed her knee. Madison was confused, because it felt good, but in a weird way in places she didn't expect it to. Her teachers and her parents always said adults shouldn't touch you, but what if it felt good? Her brain bounced back and forth between right and wrong like a ping pong ball. *I'm supposed to stop this, I think. But it's Bobby, everyone loves him, I'm supposed to respect him.* While she agonized over what was happening to her, he was sliding his hands upwards over her thigh.

The back door to the reception hall swung open.

Bobby jumped off the bench and headed for the smoker, where he was in charge of smoking the brisket for the day. She cracked her knuckles and let her hands fall to her lap. Mr. Granger walked toward them, a big smile on his face.

"Hey, Bobby, got you a little woman to help out in the kitchen, huh?" he said.

"She's not too bad." Bobby laughed and nodded. He turned his gaze toward her, and she stared down at her shoes, not knowing how to respond.

"I just came out to get some beans to take inside," Mr. Granger said. "Got any ready for me?" He held his plate forward.

Bobby slopped some beans onto the plate, and Mr. Granger headed back toward the door. Madison ran to the door and held it open for him, intending to follow him inside. She was suffocating in all these conflicting feelings, and something inside her knew Bobby wasn't done with her. What would he have done if he hadn't been interrupted? If she stayed out here, alone with him—she wasn't ready to find out.

"Hey, kiddo, why don't you stick around out here and help me for a bit?" Bobby called out.

Her stomach rose and fell like pizza dough being tossed at a pizzeria. It wobbled and threatened to come out of her throat. She looked at Mr. Granger, willing him to take her inside.

"Yeah, you go ahead, hon. I've got this." Mr. Granger stepped over the threshold, and Madison let the door close behind him.

"Now, come over here, and let's finish our talk," Bobby said. Madison took her time making her way back to the bench, flicking her eyes to the door, silently begging someone to come through again. But nobody did.

Madison started to sit, and Bobby reached up and pulled her into his lap instead. The two of them were hidden there on the side of the church. Nobody inside would know.

His hands found their way underneath the hem of her tank top, one hand on each side of her ribcage. She felt rough, scratchy, calluses slide up her chest as he brought his hands to her breasts.

She wanted to scream, she wanted to cry, to kick, to fight. But she felt weak. This was a respected man. And she was a child. Maybe this was how things worked. It *did* feel good, she couldn't deny that anymore. But it *shouldn't*. She was so confused. She was told her whole life how grown up she looked and acted. Maybe this was part of that.

Instead, she closed her eyes and felt tears streak slowly down her cheeks. She felt his breath on the back of her neck. He grunted with each exhalation. He scared her when he suddenly shoved her off his lap.

"Come over here, behind the shed," he

said. The Brother Bobby voice he'd used moments ago with Mr. Granger was gone. Now it was gruff, urgent, husky.

"I don't know, I think I should go back inside and see if—"

"No, I said get your ass over here." He grabbed her and dragged her to the side of the shed. "Get down there before I lose it."

Lose it?

He shoved her down, hard, so she was kneeling in the gravel around the small building. He unzipped his pants and exposed himself to her. Tiny pebbles and sharp stones stuck in her knees and left tiny scrapes.

"Get to work, kid," he said, grabbing her by the head.

"Was that your first encounter with Mr. Caine? On the bench behind the shed?" the detective asked.

"I'm sorry?" Madison wasn't sure how he knew about the bench.

"You were just saying the two of you had a conversation on the picnic bench."

"Oh, yes, we did." She had no idea she'd been talking, but she must have. "That wasn't the first time we met. He's been a member there for a long time. But that was the first time something weird happened."

"How many times would you say you had encounters with Mr. Caine?"

"I don't remember. That twenty years ago."

"I don't need an exact count. Ballpark. Six? Eight? A dozen?"

Madison felt pressured. She flicked her eyes back over to Cricket. Hailey again thought she was looking to her for support.

"It doesn't have to be exact," she said. "We just need to know if it was habitual or a onetime thing."

Cricket held up all ten fingers.

"I'd say it was around ten times, I guess? No less than seven or eight, for sure. I wasn't exactly counting them each time it happened."

"No, no of course you weren't. I'm sorry I have to ask these questions, but they only get more difficult from here, so you need to prepare yourself. If you can't handle it, we can stop."

"Detective, can I ask you something?"

"Sure, anything."

"Have you ever worked a case like this before? Sexual assault on children?"

He looked down at his pad, and his cheeks flushed. Madison looked toward Hailey and would swear under oath Hailey grinned and nodded, as if saying "get him."

"Well, no, nothing like this. Usually, I'm on robberies, stolen vehicles, things like that. Our town has never seen anything this scale. Why do you ask?"

"Because you would never tell a victim she can 'prepare herself' for this line of questioning. You would understand there is no preparation. There's nothing you can say or do here that's going to make this any easier. So please, don't talk to me like I'm a child or some sad wife getting her ass beat somewhere that you need to patronize to make talk. I came here to talk, and I will. But you'll let me do it however I see fit."

Cricket jumped up and down and clapped her hands. The detectives showed no signs of hearing her.

"I understand. I apologize if I made you feel that way."

"I have sat for many years with this, *handling* this alone. Being afraid. Feeling inadequate, feeling like my purpose is to be used. I've let men, and women, walk all over me. I've cowered to authority. I've apologized for everything from the weather to our flight home being delayed this weekend."

"I'm sorry you've had to go through that."

"I don't want your sorries, or your pity, or anything else. I want you to take down my story and put the bastard away. It's that simple. But I need to do this at my pace and give you the answers I know to be truthful. I'm not under investigation here, am I?"

"Of course not," he said.

"So just ask me what you need to ask and don't worry about my feelings. I'll let you know if and when I need to stop."

"Yes, ma'am. Then let's get down to it."

Cricket walked away from Hailey, rounded the corner of the desk, and wrapped her arms around Madison. She knew it wasn't real, but she felt the warmth, the pressure, the comfort.

The two of them could do this. They were about to put everybody in their places.

***

The interview continued for three long hours. Madison was peppered with questions both banal and complex and answered each one the best she could. When the answers needed to be descriptive, she ran into roadblocks.

"Can you tell us exactly how he abused

you?"

She looked at Cricket, and the little girl nodded.

Madison gave a short answer, to the point. It wasn't good enough.

"Mrs. Campbell, I need to know exactly what you remember. I know it can't be easy, but I need the details. Every last one you remember."

I need the details.

Madison and Cricket locked eyes, and Madison watched the little girl's entire demeanor change. Her eyes narrowed; her chin dipped closer to her chest. Madison saw the muscles work around her jaw. Cricket bit down on her lower lip and began gnashing and chewing until blood trickled down her chin.

I need the details.

"Mrs. Campbell? Can I get you something? Some water?"

Madison didn't respond. She couldn't take her eyes off the girl. Off *herself.*

Cricket's fingers began to grow long, the ends sharpened into barbed points, like fishhooks straightened out. Thick, black twigs, like long insect legs, broke through her rib cage and from her shoulder blades. Madison felt pains, like pinched nerves, shoot through her own neck and shoulders. Cricket's limbs crunched and crackled, like when Madison and Clay hiked through the woods near their house, stepping on branches and dead leaves. There were six or eight in all; Madison didn't take the time to count.

Cricket's new legs—arms, whatever they were—slid up the arms of Detective Hall's uniform. They moved like snakes, graceful, hypnotic. They slid over his head, around it, sizing up their prey. They coiled around and around his throat, like a boa feeling out its prey before it tightens for the kill.

Madison looked at Hailey, who had the pity mask on again. Detective Hall was watching her as if she were a bomb. Cricket was laser-focused on Hall—hunger, anger, and sadness somehow all on her face at once.

"Mrs. Campbell, is there something—"

The legs wrapped tighter, cutting off Hall's airway. Madison sat frozen. The detective began to choke, cough, and sputter. His face turned purple, and spittle dotted his legal pad, making black ink ponds where he'd made his few notes.

"Stop," Madison whispered, looking at Cricket. Hailey's gaze turned toward Madison, and the pity melted into something else—concern? Fear?

Cricket eased up, but only enough to allow the detective to breathe. She continued to hold a grip.

"Sorry," he said, still coughing and wheezing. "I must have swallowed wrong." He reached for his coffee and took a swig, realizing too late it was still piping hot. He began to cough all over again, and Cricket giggled.

"I'll get you some water, sir," Hailey said, leaving the interview room.

"Mrs. Campbell, do you mind—" He was overcome with coughs again. "Do you mind if I step out a moment and recover?"

"Sure, go ahead."

"Will you be okay here?" His chest was whistling.

"I'll be fine, thank you."

"I'll bring you some water, if you like."

"Yes, please and thank you."

The detective stood, and Cricket released her hold. Her limbs retracted back into her body, giving her the appearance of a normal child again. He exited the room, closing the door.

You can't do that, Madison sent to Cricket.

He wanted details.

I know, but it's not the same, she responded.

How do you know?

Because he's trying to help us. He isn't like them.

They're all the same, Cricket sent, then fell into Hailey's chair. She crossed her arms like a petulant child who didn't get candy on a trip to the grocery store.

Not all. Clay's not like that.

I guess. Cricket twirled her hair.

We have to answer these questions if you want to put him away. She couldn't believe she was having this ... *conversation* ... with her childhood self. Madison Campbell was sitting inside an interview room in her hometown police department talking down an imaginary version of herself that just tried to kill the detective who was trying to help.

It *was* imaginary. It had to be. But there was something about the timing, the way the detective choked and coughed at the exact moment Cricket squeezed, that was unsettling. Did Cricket have some kind of power over this time in her life? Did Madison?

Before she could answer herself, the detectives came back into the room. Detective

184

Hall's face was returning to a normal shade of flesh, and Hailey smiled down at her.

"Okay, Mrs. Campbell," Hall said. "I'm sorry about that. Can I ask you something?"

"That's why we're here, right?" Madison asked back.

"Yes, ma'am, it is." He grinned. "I was just wondering, before I started coughing, you looked like you'd gone somewhere, in your mind. Were you trying to remember? Or did something else come up?"

"Something else."

"Can you share that with me?"

Might as well. In for a penny, in for a pound.

"There were people who knew what was going on when it was going on," Madison said.

"Is that so?" Hall sat up straight and picked up his pen.

"Yes. And there was a man, he used to ask me ..." She looked back at Cricket, and the child turned away from her, facing the corner. "He used to ask me for details. He wanted to know how it felt, what I thought, what Bobby and I did. When you kept saying you wanted details ..."

"I am so sorry, Mrs. Campbell."

"It's fine."

"It's not fine. Are you comfortable giving me names? These people may have been in on everything else Caine was up to. Can you share that with me?"

Madison glanced at Cricket, who gave her a thumbs-up.

"Dennis Haines."

"And he had direct knowledge of you being abused by Mr. Caine?"

She looked at Cricket. After a beat, the lit-

185

tle girl nodded. Cricket walked over to Madison and rested her hands on the table. She gave a small nod.

"Yes, he did. And he did nothing."

Cricket disappeared.

***

After three hours of questions, tears, and anger, the interview ended. The detectives thanked her for her time and promised her everything would be okay.

At the end of the interview, Detective Hall informed her there was no longer a statute of limitations on child sexual assault. Even twenty years later, if she chose to, she could file her own charges. Did she want to do that?

Cricket reappeared then. Madison looked to her for guidance—*did* they want to? They were a team now, and it wasn't all up to Madison. She had to do what was best for both of them. Cricket didn't hesitate; she nodded her head up and down so fast Madison was afraid for her little neck. There was no question. She smiled, and the little girl smiled back. They were doing this. She agreed, and Detective Hall promised to have the charges drawn up within the hour.

"There's enough here that he will die in prison," Hall said.

She allowed the surge of relief to swallow her while Hailey walked her to the car. The detective took out her phone and typed in a web address. It was a way for Madison to keep up with what was going on with Bobby, to be able to see public records related to the case, where he was, and so on.

"You'll have to create your own account, but I'm logged into mine so I can show you. So, you just tap here." Tap. "And then here, and then in this box, type his name in." Tap. Tap. Tap. "And search—*shit.*"

Madison looked at the screen, and just like that, the surge or relief betrayed her and spit her back out onto the hot concrete parking lot.

"What the fuck?" Madison's body went cold.

"I'm so sorry," Hailey said.

Madison could see the words **BOND MADE** next to Bobby's name.

"You have all this evidence, he'll die in prison, but he's out walking around right now? Is he *here?*" Her stomach leapt to her heart, trying to drown her, and it beat faster and faster trying to stay afloat. Anxiety struck a match and touched it to her lungs, engulfing them in fire like a dry forest kindling in the summer.

Madison's eyes swept the building. They traveled over each window, narrowing and trying to focus on the dark panes. She looked for all possible exits. She felt herself lace her keys between her fingers, as she had many times before, in an effort to make deadly claws.

Hailey grabbed her shoulders, and Madison screamed.

"Madison, he's *not* here. He was booked into the main facility. He's not here. You're safe."

She looked at Hailey and then back at the building.

Cricket was standing at the front door. She walked inside, and Madison thought she saw movement in the windows. Finally, Cricket came back through the doors. She nodded at Madison and made an "OK" sign with her fingers.

Cricket was always the brave one.

"He got out on the first charges. Yours haven't hit yet. When they do, he's headed right back in."

"When mine hit, he goes back in?"

"Yes," Hailey answered. "And hopefully, the judge sets a very high bond, and we don't do this again. Either way, there's been a protective order issued for you and the other victim. He's not allowed anywhere near you or your family. If you see him, you call us. We're here to protect you."

She should have been comforted by this, and she was, a little bit. But mostly, she wanted to laugh. These people clearly did not know Bobby Caine. No piece of paper was going to tell him what to do. She was not safe because it was in black and white in a folder somewhere or out in the cloud.

Don't worry, Cricket said. *I will protect you. We don't need them.*

Madison's stomach crept back where it belonged, and the flames in her lungs were doused. Bobby didn't even know she'd come forward yet. He probably didn't even remember her. She wasn't as special as he'd said, there were many more like her, so maybe she'd slipped his mind.

Of course, she wouldn't be forgotten for long. Once Hall showed up with these charges, she'd be front and center in Bobby Caine's life once again.

Hailey left her once she'd calmed down enough to drive. Madison turned the radio on and raised the volume. The volume lowered again on its own. She looked at Cricket, who was sitting in the passenger seat, arms crossed over her chest, staring out the window.

Ever the petulant child, she thought.

"Cricket," she said, turning the volume back up. "I know it doesn't seem like much, but we did a good thing today. It was hard as hell, but I think we're going to get somewhere if we work together. We'll get through it."

Cricket didn't respond.

"Fine, you can sit over there and sulk, I'm okay with that. We just had a shitty afternoon, but I still think it's going to end up somewhere good. Our only other choice is to catastrophize and imagine him being free and us still being cast aside. I don't know about you, but I don't want to spend my days like that. We have enough anxiety and shit we deal with; no need to create more."

Madison noticed Cricket's fingers tapping to the beat of the music. Then she saw one of her sneakers bouncing up and down a tiny bit. Madison sang along to the tunes, loud and feeling good about herself and what she'd just done. Cricket joined in, quietly at first, and by the time they were pulling into the driveway, she was shouting lyrics as loud as Madison was.

Things were looking up.

***

"I know this is the worst possible time," Clay said. His suitcase was on the bed, and he was hanging a suit in a garment bag. "I can ask them for time off."

"No, you can't. If you do, you'll have to

explain why. I'm not ready for your colleagues to know what we're dealing with. I'm trying my best to stay anonymous in all of this. I don't want anyone asking you questions."

"I'll just tell them it's a family emergency. People don't usually ask too many questions about stuff like that."

"No," Madison repeated, shaking her head. She always felt better having Clay in the house versus being alone. This time was a little different because Cricket was here. Madison felt like she was safer with the little girl than she would be with anyone else on the planet. "You need to go. We have to live a normal life, go about our routines. This is something from *my* past, and I can deal with it. I'm a big girl, Clay."

"I know." He laid his garment bag down flat on the bed. "But I want to be here for you. It's not like you asked for any of this." He sat down beside her and took her hand.

"I'll be fine. This could go on for months. We can't live the next however many of them sitting on the couch thinking about it. Besides, I've got Cricket."

Clay tilted his head like a confused puppy dog.

"Cricket? Who's that?"

Three weeks had passed since Madison's police station interview. Bobby was arrested on her charges, booked, and released on bond again. So far, he'd made no attempt to contact her. Cricket hung around the house most days. She and Madison played games, watched movies, and chatted about life. Cricket had become her best friend. Of course, Clay couldn't see her, and Madison never told him about her. She couldn't now either, or he'd think she'd gone over the edge. She couldn't stand any more coddling.

"She's my character in that video game I play. You know, the one where you always end up in a corner, smacking brick walls with a low-level dagger?" She poked him in the ribs and laughed. Madison played her games every day, it was her way to escape the world around her and get lost somewhere else. Clay couldn't remember which buttons did what.

"Ah, okay, the elf girl thing?"

Madison rolled her eyes.

"She's not an elf girl *thing*. She's an elf. And I named her Cricket. She and I will pass the time while you're on your trip. It'll be fine. How long will you be gone for this one?"

"Three weeks, four at most."

Madison loved being married. She loved having Clay there day in and day out, to laugh and joke, help with chores, and live the day to day ups and downs of life. But she was also more of a solo creature, so she was looking forward to having a few weeks to herself.

She helped him finish packing and kissed him at the door before he left in his Uber for the airport. Once the car pulled away from the house, she closed and locked her front door. When she made it back to the living room, Cricket was already sitting there, waiting.

There hadn't been many chances for Cricket and Madison to be together uninterrupted. Since everything started happening, Clay was glued to her side. She knew he was afraid, and she loved him for it, but she'd been craving time to talk to Cricket. Madison wanted an explanation.

"So, let's talk," she said to Cricket. The little girl turned sideways on the couch, crossing her legs as if preparing to meditate. Madison mirrored her actions, now facing her on the couch.

"I know why you're here; I think. It's some sort of post-traumatic stress disorder response, right? You're not really here, my brain is conjuring you up as a way to deal with all of this, right?"

Cricket shrugged.

"I can accept that, that you're my imagination or whatever. That much makes sense. What I don't understand is why the detective choked in the interview room."

This time Cricket grinned along with the shrug.

Was I always that creepy? Madison asked herself.

"How could he have felt your—whatever they were. I don't know if they were legs or tentacles or what they were, but how could the detective feel those wrap around his neck? Enough for him to choke? Was it a coincidence?"

Cricket didn't respond.

"I don't understand. You *can't* be real. You can't have that kind of power over things—"

Cricket leapt off the couch and ran for the front door. She looked out the window, and her body began to shake. Madison could feel the vibrations in the air. It made her think of being at concerts and standing in front of the huge amplifiers the bands used. As the bass flew out of the speaker, you could feel it hit your body before you heard it.

"What is it?"

Cricket's face flushed with fire. Steam rose from her scalp and escaped in thin, wispy tendrils from her ears. Madison felt the vibrations the girl was sending and heat in her own scalp. She reached up to touch it. Cricket pointed at the small window near the top of the front door.

Madison stood on her tiptoes and peeked.

A blue truck was parked in front of her house, pulled alongside the curb. A man sat at the steering wheel in a hat and dark glasses. The window was down. She couldn't make out his face in the shade, but she knew.

"It's him, isn't it?" she asked Cricket.

Cricket walked *through* the door. Madison raised a hand to her mouth to stifle a yell. She didn't want the man to know she was inside and afraid. She watched Cricket walk down the path toward the curb, stopping a foot or so from the truck. *Don't do it,* she sent to the little girl. *Don't hurt him. Just scare him off. We should call the pol—*

Cricket sent out a shriek that rattled Madison's teeth. She wrenched the door open, pulling it so wide, Madison heard metal crunching from inside. The man inside tried to jump out, but his feet failed him. His back slid down the runners and caught himself before his ass hit the ground. He spun in circles, flailing his arms, trying to figure out what the hell just happened. His glasses bounced around on his fat, oily nose and slipped off onto the concrete. She saw him clear as day.

Bobby Lawrence Caine, standing in her front yard. She was supposed to call the police. So much for that piece of paper—that *order* to stay away from her. But something inside her wanted to see what Cricket did first. What was two more minutes?

Bobby jumped back into the cab of his truck, reached for the door, and changed his mind. He didn't try for the seatbelt; he reached for the gearshift instead. All six windows in the pickup exploded. Glass flew through the air like fireworks sparks, showering down on Bobby and the street. Madison was pretty sure he was screaming in tongues, just like the folks from the church. Cricket picked up a chunk of glass and squeezed. That same second, Madison felt a sharp sting in her palm. She looked down and found a blooming dot of crimson.

NO! Madison sent.

Cricket froze.

Don't kill him. We need justice first. This is too easy for him. And it's in my yard, in front of my house, and it's not gonna look good for us if you do this. Let him go.

Cricket brought the glass down anyway but stopped once the point broke the skin on Bobby's neck. She let out another animal cry, and Madison swore Bobby heard it. His entire body tensed up, his eyes squeezed shut, and he reached for his ears. He finally got hold of the gearshift and sped off, open doors and all. Madison caught one last glimpse of his face and saw pure terror. He fled the scene without looking back.

Madison opened the door, and Cricket made sweeping gestures with her hands. The shards of glass in the yard and street gathered as if swept by a broom, and Cricket eased them down the curb drain. Madison looked at her neighbors' homes, waiting for one of the nosy folks to open their doors and ask questions.

They can't hear anything I do, Madison heard inside her head.

I think he did, Madison responded.

Because I wanted him to.

"Thank you for stopping," she said.

There was a long pause before she received Cricket's response.

Next time I won't.

***

Clay returned from his business trip, and life went back to normal. Months crawled along with Madison telling her story over and over to prosecutors. She had an advocate, Mathias, who walked her through every step. Cricket was always there, in the corner, looking ready to pounce.

Trial day finally arrived, and Clay, Madison, and Cricket headed for the courthouse together.

Mathias had given Madison and Clay a tour of the courthouse several weeks before. He wanted her to ask questions and feel comfortable with her surroundings, so when trial day came, she'd be somewhat familiar with the environment.

"He will be there when I testify?"

"He will. But there will be heavy police presence, and he should be in cuffs. You'll be safe. I'll be here, and Clay ..." he looked over and made eye contact with Clay, who nodded, "Clay will be here too. You can have whatever support you like. It's a public trial, but closed to the media. Any family, friends, a therapist, anyone you want is welcome to be here to support you."

Madison looked at Clay and then at Cricket.

You will be safe, Cricket echoed inside her head.

Madison was now standing in the courthouse again, ready to face her demon for the first time in decades.

The courtroom filled with faces she recognized, and some she didn't. She saw Bobby's brothers sitting in the seats behind the defense. She also saw two or three members of the church, who still stood behind him. Dennis Haines—Mr. Details—stood among them. There must not have been enough for them to go after him too. Her name hadn't been given to the public, but Bobby had it, and she was sure they knew. They stared at her as if she were a used condom in the collection plate—disgusting and shameful.

On the prosecution side, she saw what appeared to be other victims she hadn't been told about, and their families. The young girls looked the same as she felt: terrified, but somehow hopeful. They were too young to be jaded by the system, and she was jealous of that. She recognized some faces from Bobby's neighborhood; they'd recently been on the news soaking up the attention. It was fine with her. She'd rather it be their faces people saw than hers.

That was all going to end today. The anonymity she'd fought so hard for would be stripped from her, just as her sense of safety and comfort, her self-worth, her confidence was stripped from her all those years ago. It would leave her vulnerable, bloody, and raw for the media and his supporters to pick apart. Her words and emotions would be autopsied by both sides, each one using them to prove their point.

Madison felt a warm hand in the small of her back and jumped.

"Hey, honey, it's time for us to go," Clay said.

The victims were taken to separate rooms for the start of the trial. They wouldn't be allowed to observe until they'd already given their testimony. She supposed it was to keep things fair, keep witnesses honest, but it still irked her. Why should they be treated this way when all the evidence was there without their testimony in the first place? But she would acquiesce, because everything had to be done by the book.

Madison kept her eyes on the clock, not looking at Clay or Cricket. One hour and twenty-seven minutes later, Mathias opened the door.

"Okay, Madison, it's time. You ready to do this?"

"As ready as I'm going to be, I think."

She stood and hugged Clay. He put his hand on her shoulders and brought his forehead to hers. "You've got this. I'll be right there. You look at me if you need to. Nobody else has to be in that courtroom but me and you, if it makes you feel better. You are the strongest woman I know, and there's not a doubt in my mind you've got this."

"And there's always an out," Mathias interrupted. "If you need to stop at any time, you say the word, and we'll get you off the stand."

Madison looked at Cricket.

She heard Cricket's voice inside her head. *Remember the letter? The one you wrote to me in therapy? 'He will face judgment one day,' you said. 'And we will be there. Holding hands, twirling, laughing.' This is it. We put him down today, once and for all.*

"Mad?"

Madison looked back at Clay. "We got this," she said.

She took Cricket's hand and followed Mathias to the courtroom.

***

She walked through a door near the judge's bench, and her eyes were pulled to Bobby's like a magnet to steel.

Her body filled with ice water. Her hands trembled, and she could actually *feel* the color drain from her face. She stood frozen in the doorway, unable to take another step.

I can't do this, she sent to Cricket.

You can, and you will.

I'm afraid of him. I'm not allowed to ever tell. He'll hurt me if I do. I have to take everything back.

Madison felt like she'd stepped back in time. She was standing in front of him, in a closet in the church. He'd just finished having his way with her when he stopped and grabbed her by the chin.

"You can't tell anybody about this, don't you forget that."

"I won't."

"You'll fuck everything up if you do. I'll just as soon kill you before I let you ruin my life. No pussy is worth that. You keep your mouth shut, and everything will be just fine."

He slapped her on the cheek.

"Yes, sir," she said, tears welling in her eyes.

No! We're not going back there! Cricket's shout reverberated inside Madison's head. *We were afraid, but we don't have to be anymore. We lived all these years afraid of him, afraid of everything and everyone, but once we saw his face—I came back so we could put the fucker down, and that's what we're going to do. We're not scared little thirteen-year-olds anymore. We have the upper hand, and you're going to take it!*

Cricket grabbed her by the hand, and a fire lit inside her. Her hands grew sweaty, her face flushed, and her heart took off at a quickening pace. The fear leapt out of her like an exorcised demon—she swore she *saw* it leave. In its place was an unrelenting rage.

This was it. This was their time.

"Madison? Madison?" Mathias was repeating her name, whispering it in her ear.

"Sorry," she said.

"Never be sorry. We knew this part wouldn't be easy."

Madison allowed him to lead her to the stand, where she raised her hand and took an oath.

She spent the next hour on the stand, reiterating her story for what felt like the millionth time. She detailed all the disgusting, violent, horrible things he did to her mind and her body. Everything went well with the prosecution. They were on her side.

Then it was time for the defense to ask questions, and they were not on her side. They did everything they could to undermine her testimony and convince the jury she was a liar. Throughout the testimony, Madison watched Bobby.

"Now, Mrs. Campbell, you said Mr. Caine assaulted you ten times?"

"Yes."

Bobby shook his head, shock on his face, looking at his supporters. He made as if he was just as shocked as they were.

"And you were thirteen?"

"Twelve, thirteen, somewhere around there. I don't remember exact dates. It was a long time ago."

"Is it possible you mistook Mr. Caine's concern and guidance after the death of your parents as something it was not? Did you mistake a hug or special attention to mean you were in some kind of relationship with Mr. Caine?"

Bobby looked at her, the corners of his mouth fighting a battle to smile. He raised one of his bloated hands to his mouth to hide it.

"Absolutely not!" she said. "He did things to me I did not ask for, and they were far beyo—"

"A yes or no, please, Mrs. Campbell," his defense attorney said.

Madison looked for Cricket. The little girl was walking around the room, drawing ovals around people. When the shape was complete, they sat in what looked like glass domes, or bubbles of some kind. She drew the shapes over Clay, Mathias, the other victims, and their families.

What are you doing? she sent.

Cricket didn't respond. She continued drawing the domes over a handful of people, about fifteen in all.

When Madison was finally finished testifying, she stepped down and sat with Clay in the courtroom. She would now be allowed to hear the rest of the evidence and testimonies. The next person was called, and Madison almost fell into Clay's lap with shock.

"The defense calls Bobby Lawrence Caine, your honor."

Bobby turned in her direction, grinned, and headed for the stand.

***

He swore the same oath she did and took his seat. His answers were nothing less than expected by Madison and the other victims.

"I never touched her. She was a child, and she came to me for guidance. That's how we do things in the church, we help each other."

Madison watched Cricket. The little girl walked past the courtroom exits, tapping her hands along the door jambs. Each time she tapped, a small bubble appeared. It reminded Madison of insect eggs. The membrane was cloudy, but she could see small movements and wiggles underneath.

What are you doing?

Cricket continued on to each door and window, leaving the sacs. They were spaced about a foot apart, from the baseboard to the top corner of the door, across the top, and back down the other side.

"It was clear she was a troubled child. The loss of her parents affected her in a deep way. I should have gathered more members of the church rather than taking it all on my shoulders."

Madison looked at Clay, who blurred as her eyes filled with tears. *What a burden you took on, Bobby. Such sacrifices you made for me.* Bile rose in her throat, and she forced it back down.

Cricket made her way to the front of the courtroom and stood in front of the judge's bench. She faced the crowd and brought her arms up parallel to the floor. Her palms faced forward, hands open, fingers splayed.

I don't know what you're planning, but don't mess this up, Madison sent.

I know what I'm doing.

She brought her hands together in front of her chest and laced her fingers. As she did, the sacs opened, some cracking like eggs, others bursting like water balloons.

Something's hatching, Madison thought, surprised by her lack of fear. Instead, she was full of wonderment, full of anticipation. *Where is this going?* The sacs on the doors produced long, thick, eel-like creatures. They were glossy, as if covered with slime, but did not leave tracks. They crawled across the wood and laced under and over each other.

The sacs around the windows also hatched, producing the same type of creatures, except these were transparent, allowing sunlight to shine through. People couldn't see Cricket or the things she conjured, but they *would* notice if the room went dark. Cricket thought of everything, it seemed.

Once the exits were sealed, she thrust her hands in front of her, creating tiny duplicates of the others. They were only inches long and slimmer than a pencil. They split into groups and headed for the officers in the courtroom. Madison watched them climb up the officers' legs, finding their weapons. They slid down into the holsters and didn't come back up. Others wrapped themselves around cans of pepper spray, blocking the nozzles.

Madison's jaw went slack, and her eyes widened as she realized what Cricket's next moves would be. *She's expecting some sort of fight.*

Abso-fucking-lutely I am, Cricket responded.

The next words out of Bobby Lawrence Caine's mouth lit the fuse.

"She threw herself at me. She always wore those short shorts, tank tops. She always wanted to talk about sexual things. She tried to pull my hands to her breast once, and I pushed her away. I'm only guilty of not asking for help."

Lies! Cricket's voice boomed in Madison's head, amplified. Madison raised her hands to her head and ducked, screaming. Everyone in the courtroom looked in her direction. When she sat up, she saw the smile on Bobby's face. Madison was proving his point. The jury would eat it up.

Except it didn't matter. This case wasn't going to jury.

Madison watched as Cricket sprouted more legs. They were the same legs that tried to choke Detective Hall many weeks ago. Except this time, they lifted Cricket off the ground. Four thick branches, each covered in thorns, held her at least five feet high. Six more broke free from her back and shoulders, rising toward the ceiling.

The courtroom was as silent as a corpse lying in a coffin. Everyone was still looking at her.

Cricket sent her limbs to Bobby. She raised him from his seat and slammed him against the wall, creating a dent. People in the courtroom began to scream, some running for exits that would not open. Others were trapped inside the domes Cricket created for them. They banged against the air; confusion painted on their faces.

Madison turned to Clay, who was trying to fight his way out of his own invisible bubble. She placed her hands where his were on the other side. "You're going to be okay," she said. "I'm safe, don't worry about me. This will all be over soon. I love you."

Clay stared back, confused.

The officers pulled their weapons, scanning the room, but had nothing and no one to fire at.

Cricket released Bobby, and he fell to the floor. He scrambled to his feet, but Cricket was faster, and she sent more eels. They created a cocoon around him, disallowing his arms and legs movement. When Bobby opened his mouth to scream, an eel slid its way between his lips and into his throat.

"Stop this!" Madison yelled aloud. "Cricket, stop!"

Cricket lowered her feet to the ground, raising her limbs to her sides. Bobby's supporters, whom she had not protected with domes, were fighting the doors, trying to pull them open. Officers were trying to shoot at the locks, but their weapons would not fire. Nobody could see the wall of creatures Cricket had sealed the doors with. They still had hope.

Two of Cricket's limbs slid along the floor and found Bobby's brothers. They crawled up their bodies and wrapped themselves around the men's heads. Madison could no longer see their faces.

But she heard the *crack* of their skulls caving in.

She saw the blood pour through the gaps between the layers of limbs. Their bodies went limp, and they slid from Cricket's grasp.

When they hit the ground, Madison's eyes traveled up their bodies to what should have been their heads. Instead, her eyes landed on what looked like roadkill—like an unlucky raccoon crossed the wrong highway at the wrong time and was flattened by dump truck tires. She couldn't discern any facial features. It was ground hamburger meat with bits of bone.

And so much blood.

Cricket left the bodies and went after the church members. She split their torsos open from left to right and neck to groin. Madison recognized the shape of the cross as she watched the men's entrails spill from their bellies. The center of the cross was large enough for Madison to see the heart of Dennis Haines. It beat three or four times, then ceased.

The only people in the courtroom were those left in domes, the officers, and Bobby. Cricket looked toward the door that led to the judge's chambers. The eels parted, and it opened. She waved her hand, and the domes lowered.

"We have to get the fuck out of here," Clay said, grabbing Madison by the shoulders.

"I can't," she said. "But you have to. All of

you have to. Leave me with him."

"What?" Clay's voice cracked, and she could see him questioning her sanity in his eyes.

"Just go. Leave me here!"

Clay started to argue. Cricket intervened, lifting him and sending him to the door. She grabbed Mathias with another leg. She pushed them through, slammed the door, and sealed it again.

Now it was Cricket, Madison, and Bobby. The moment Madison had yearned for since she was twelve years old.

Cricket lifted Bobby upright and held him off the ground. She brought him over to Madison.

Say everything you need to say, Cricket sent. *Get it all out right now. You won't get another chance.*

This was it. Bobby was finally going to pay for what he'd done to her, and to the others. *The others.*

Why didn't you leave the others? Don't they get to have their say? They're broken, too.

Too young, Cricket said. *This way, he will pay, and they will be able to go on. They don't need to see this. It would only damage them more. We are doing this for them, and for us, and for any who didn't come forward.*

Madison could handle this, and Cricket knew it. She knew it because she *was* Madison. They were the same. Cricket was a tough child, swallowing everything thrown at her. It had its side effects—her anxieties, fear, depression, low self-worth—but she persevered. So many times, she wanted to give up. She wanted to swallow the pills, cut her wrists, hang from the ceiling. But she never did.

Madison may have forgotten her strength for a while, but Cricket lived inside her, and she came back at the right time to remind her.

"Hi, Bobby," Madison said.

Bobby tried to scream.

"Oh, I'm sorry, let me help you with that." She looked at Cricket, who made a motion with her hands. The eel removed itself from Bobby's mouth, breaking teeth and tearing flesh on its way out.

"Let me try that again. Hi, Bobby."

"What the hell is this?"

Madison looked around the room, at the corpses on the floor, the blood on the walls. She looked back at Bobby.

"It looks like it's judgment day." She shrugged. "When I saw your face on my screen, I'm not going to lie, my heart filled with fear. But then, the more I learned about your little habit, the angrier I got. Dozens of computers and phones with child pornography on them, some that you produced yourself. Narcissistic enough to show your face. That was the nail in the coffin. If you hadn't shown your face, you *might* have gotten away with just a porn charge. But you did."

Madison sat down in a chair behind the prosecution table.

"And you weren't banking on anyone talking. You made us afraid. You thought you had power and control. And you did, for a little while. But then we spoke up. That little girl on your last video went to her mother. She beat you. And then the rest unraveled, all leading to today. To justice."

"There's nothing to judge. I didn't do anything to you."

"Now, Bobby." Madison looked at the floor and shook her head. "You know better. We were both there. It's just me and you now. You can tell the truth."

"I never would have touched you. Look at you. You were an ugly kid, and you're worse off now. I don't know how the hell you ever found a husband."

Madison flinched. This was all in line with Bobby's character; he was the innocent until you cornered him, and then he wanted to destroy you. She was surprised at how much his words still stung. *Maybe he—*

Oh no you don't! Cricket shouted. *He does not get to do this anymore!* The tiny hairs on Madison's neck and arms stood straight up. She looked at Cricket, whose face was red. *This ends now!*

"I don't think that was the right thing to say," Madison said.

Cricket forced one of Bobby's arms free. She wrapped another leg around his wrist and ripped the arm off. Blood sprayed across his face, turning the whites of his eyes pink. The end of the leg that tore the arm off began to glow orange. Madison felt the heat as Cricket reached for the gaping hole the arm left.

"Now this might hurt a little, Bobby. But we don't want you bleeding out or anything." Inside, she was conflicted. Adult Madison wanted to be terrified, wanted to be anxious, wanted to second guess everything she was doing. But little Madison—Cricket—was battling for control, and she was winning. The rage, the snark, the power ... it all felt so good.

Cricket jammed the glowing end into the hole, cauterizing the wound. Bobby screamed in pain. Smoke rose, and the acrid, yet somehow sweet, smell of flesh worked its way into Madison's nose.

"How are you doing this?" he asked her, sobbing and wheezing.

"Oh, don't you remember? I'm special. You said it yourself back then. Right after you threw me down in your truck and tore *my* body. I bled on your leather seat, remember? Of course, it wasn't near as much blood as you're leaving behind here." She gestured to the floor.

"I'm sorry, okay? Is that what you want to hear? I'm sick, and I have a problem, and I'm sorry."

Madison almost laughed at how unconvincing he sounded, at how dramatic the look on his face was. He was trying hard to sell the 'poor me' bit, but she wasn't buying.

"I need help. But I can't get help unless you let me out of here. Do that for me, kiddo. Let me out, and they'll send me away, and you'll never see me again."

Kiddo. The word echoed inside her head, and then flashbacks began to play like a movie behind her eyes.

Hey, kiddo. The two of them on the bench, his hand on her knee.

You're so beautiful, kiddo. His hand on her cheek, his thumb tracing her lips.

This is our secret, kiddo, okay? Him handing her a towel to wipe her mouth.

God-damn it, kiddo, hold still! Inside the truck.

"I'm done talking," Madison said, her

body trembling. "You will never hurt me, or any other child, ever again. It's done."

"So, you'll let me go?"

Do it, Madison sent. She stepped back to watch.

Cricket let go of Bobby, and he fell to the floor, landing on his feet. He tried to run, and Cricket let him for several feet. Inches before he got to a door, Cricket wrapped her limbs around each of his legs and his other arm and yanked him back to where he started. He was helpless, the same way she was all those years ago.

One of Cricket's eels worked its way up Bobby's pant leg. It tore a hole in the crotch, spitting out fabric until it exposed Bobby.

It's smaller than I remember, Madison thought. She watched the eel wrap itself over and over around the flaccid flesh, crushing it. Cricket grabbed the eel by the tail. It tightened its grip.

Cricket pulled.

Madison's heart filled with glee as she watched the chunk of flesh ripped from its host. Bobby's screams soothed her, in a way. To know he was the one scared, he was the one not coming back from something. Blood continued to squirt from the stump, bathing his shoes, which looked brand new. *He had to come in looking put together,* she thought. Bobby watched it, shivering, wailing. His eyes bulged and rolled around like lottery number balls before being picked. His chin fell to his chest, and he passed out. The eel carried what was left to a corner and began to feast.

Bobby was jolted awake when Cricket

cauterized the fresh wound.

"Oh good, you're awake," Madison said.

This is your last chance, Cricket sent.

"I have a few things I'd like to say before our time here is done.

"I—" Bobby began, but Cricket sealed his mouth again.

"It's rude to interrupt," Madison said. "Anyway. You really did a number on me back then, Bobby. You made it so I trusted no one. I felt like some toy everybody should get to play with until they were bored. I let myself be passed from man to man, like a broken china bowl from the Goodwill. Each of them chipped away at me, piece by piece."

She heard laughter in her head. *Much like he is now! Piece by piece!* Cricket couldn't control herself. It set Madison off into a fit, matching her snort for snort.

"Sorry about that," Madison said, trying to regain her composure. "Just realized you're kind of being chipped away too. Well, *ripped apart,* rather."

Bobby murmured something.

"What was that?" Madison asked.

Cricket slipped her limbs apart enough for Bobby to speak.

"Please, stop." Bobby said. Cricket covered his mouth again.

"*Please stop,*" Madison repeated, mocking him. "You never listened when I asked you to stop. You'd be delusional to think I'm going to listen now. You're a dead man, Bobby. Maybe in thirty seconds, maybe thirty minutes, I haven't decided."

Bobby groaned.

"Anyway, as I was saying before I was so *rudely* interrupted, *again*. I lived my life afraid of you. Afraid of all men, actually. I could be at a grocery store and have to leave my basket where it was and run out the doors because a man *looked* at me. He was probably only looking for canned beans, but my anxiety-riddled brain told me he was looking at me, sizing me up. And that was because of you."

She began to pace. "I used to check the obituaries once a month. Hoping to see your name. I once wrote a letter to my 'inner child' when I was in therapy. I told her how one day you'd get yours. And she and I would spit on your dead face and dance on your grave."

And we will, Cricket sent. *I don't want to wait anymore.*

"I suppose it's about time."

Bobby tried to speak, but Cricket wouldn't allow it.

"No?" Madison asked. "Nothing?"

Bobby continued to try. Madison looked at Cricket and nodded.

Cricket pulled at Bobby's arm and legs, finishing the quartering she'd started. Madison sat behind the prosecution table, her hands clasped in front of her. Her body did not tremble, her heart did not race. She soaked everything up, trying to commit the final scene to memory.

Bobby was probably dead once his arms and legs were gone, but it didn't matter to Cricket. She tossed his appendages aside and lifted his torso, slamming it to the floor over and over again. Madison listened as his bones shattered, imagining his insides turning to strawberry jam.

Cricket screamed and hollered the entire time, letting out years of rage and pain. She pulled Bobby's head off, smashed it as she had his brothers', and threw it onto their corpses. She jammed her limbs into his chest and stabbed him over and over, sending blood and flesh into the air to rain back down on her.

After several minutes, the room went quiet again. Cricket's limbs slid back into her small body, leaving no evidence they were there to begin with. The little girl knelt over Bobby's body, her hands on what was left of his chest. She began to sob, crying out in pain like a wounded animal.

Madison stood and walked over to her, kneeling beside her. She wrapped her arms around Cricket and pulled the girl toward her chest.

"It's okay now," she said. "We did it. It's over. We survived."

Cricket continued to wail. Madison began to shake and finally lost her composure. She wept alongside Cricket, their howls blending in harmony. They cried until their throats were raw.

Madison stood and held her hand out to Cricket. She pulled the little girl to her feet, and they looked down at Bobby's body. Madison spat. Cricket did the same.

Music began echoing inside Madison's head, sent by Cricket.

They twirled and danced, laughing and clapping their hands. Their feet splashed in the puddles of blood that once gave life to their abuser. Madison closed her eyes, listening to the music. When she opened them again, Cricket was gone, and Madison was dancing alone.

She was whole again.

PATCHWORK

DESIREE BYARS

Acknowledgments

A number of people had a hand in making this dream of mine become a reality. If I have missed you, please know you aren't forgotten. It's not easy to condense a lifetime of thanks into a handful of paragraphs. Everyone in my life is loved and appreciated. It took a village to raise this child, and I'm grateful for all of you.

First and foremost, Stephen, who read all the words and used a red crayon to put me in my place. You always come through, and without you pushing me, even when I was yelling at you, I would have never made it here. You put up with more than anyone else, and still love me through the good and the bad. You sacrificed a lot through this process and never complained. You are my sunshine. Life has been a journey, and I'm still glad I got on the roller coaster!

My mom, Melinda, and my brother, Justin. I love you guys with my whole heart, and you have all my thanks for your support and for putting up with me. Having a Desiree isn't always easy, but thus far, you have kept me around, so I love you both.

Dad, I did it. Wish you were here to see it.

Mike Lane, my partner-in-crime, my constant beta reader, my cantaloupehead. Without you, this book would have been so much harder. You pushed me when I needed it, cussed me when I needed it, and encouraged me all along the way. You put up with my garbage all hours of the day and night; you don't let me wallow in doubt, and I owe you so much. You are the GOAT in every respect. Now, if you'll leave some comments on this acknowledgment and tell me where to expand, I'll get right to it. But you already know.

Michele Bachman, I don't have enough words to thank you for all you have done. The year 2019 was successful in large part because of you. You're my cheerleader, my calmer-downer, the only person who laughs at every single one of my stupid jokes. I am so lucky to have found you and hope we are in each other's lives for many years to come.

Denise Ingham, you know what you've done for me. You were just as much a part of this as anyone else, if not more so. Thank you.

Lisa Vasquez, my life boss, my all-in-one. Nobody on the planet works harder than you do. Thank you for believing in me and Bailey and everybody else I've created. I am so glad the convention gods threw us together. I cannot use enough words here to tell you what you mean to me. And please don't write "expand on this" in the margins here. This is it, all you get. Use your imagination.

The Stitched Smile Publications staff and fellow authors, you guys are amazing! You welcomed me with open arms from the very beginning, and each of you had a hand in where I've ended up. I owe you many thanks.

Lisa Lee Tone, my editor, who shredded this work with all her talons and found all the many places to make it better. I believe in her work and am proud to have her on my side, helping me turn this into the best work it can be. She even edited my acknowledgments, she's that dedicated. Love her to pieces.

Jae Mazer, without you, I'd still be hiding

my words in my head or in my laptop. Thank you for taking the time to talk to me at my first convention and for pushing me to get my story out. You giving me those few minutes of your time made all the difference, and I am forever grateful for the path you helped set me on.

Holly Baker, my sister, my best friend from almost cradle to grave, I love you and thank you for being my ride or die. The one who rides the Wonkavator with me and dances with Oompa Loompas. The one who licks walls with me so we can taste the raspberries and snozberries. The one who has been through all the highs and all the very lows with me, tears, laughter, and love.

Elizabeth Bogunovich, the girl who went from my little cousin to one of my very best friends. The girl who I used to guide through life now guides me and has been a rock in ways she will never know. I am so proud of who you have become and thank you for being there when I've needed you! Jon gets a mention here so he doesn't yell at me later. I kid. He's a keeper.

Allyson Bogunovich, I love you to pieces. Your spirit, humor, and kindness make my heart swell. I'm so proud of who you're becoming and can't wait to see where you go!

Alberto Garcia, Jr., who went from hating my guts to being one of my most dear friends. The guy who spent hours and hours with me, shooting zombies and listening to my incessant chatter about life, and who doesn't get too mad when I scare him with all the things he hates. Also, he leaves me behind in hordes of zombies to fend for myself—so does he really deserve this acknowledgment?

Pam Brown, I miss you, and I miss taco

Tuesdays on Wednesdays. I'm so glad we found each other. You're a light in my life, always making me smile, always going to bat for me, and letting me slowly turn you over to the dark side. I love you!

Heather Puppa, always ready to whisk me away to lunch and help me get some breathing room. You, too, have been there for me in many ways in the last year, and I appreciate you more than you will ever know.

Keith Williams, the Master to my Grasshopper. You were the first adult who had real faith in my skills (other than parents, who are kind of obligated). You took me on when nobody else wanted to and taught me so much about the newspaper world and life in general. I miss days of riding around in the Camaro, blasting music, and laughing the workday away. I'm glad we were able to reconnect again, and you've been an integral part in this last year too. Thank you for teaching me.

Maximiliano Ayala, I could not have gotten through these last several months without you. You know what you did, and I thank you from the bottom of my heart. I don't know how you put up with me sometimes, but you did, and you are a wonderful human being. The world needs more like you.

Last, but certainly not least, a wee little shout out to Elle Rodriguez and her mother, Sierra Jimenez. I am so thankful to have you in my life! Welcome to the family!

Desiree Byars is a fan of all things horror. She enjoys reading, video games, and movies. She lives with her husband and several rescue animals.

www.facebook.com/DesireeByarsAuthor
scriptorcorruptus.com